Teardrops Know My Name

To Artine,

Wishing you an abundant joy & success!

Thank you for your support!

Best regards,

dalia floren

11 - 18 - 15

Teardrops Know My Name
By Dalia Florea

Teardrops Know My Name

Published by Dalia Florea

© 2014 Dalia Florea

For questions about this book contact Dalia Florea

www.daliafloreabooks.com

Cover design by Visual Luxe

Editing by Lori Draft (Creationscolors)

Acknowledgements

I thank God for giving me the power to believe in my passion and pursue my dreams.

To my children Bruce and Kimberly, thank you for always cheering me on. Love you both so very much.

Prologue

Tardiness . . . She hated it, but she was going to be late.

She sprinted to the car like she'd been training for the Olympic two hundred meter dash. Keys in hand, she pushed the remote to unlock the door. She was more than twenty-five feet or so away from the car, but anything that would save her seconds would help her beat minutes of traffic. She mentally retraced her exodus from the house . . . she had her phone, the address, and her wallet. That was all she needed. Not the makeup she was accustomed to wearing or even the jewelry that would have made her outfit complete. It was all she could do to pop in the shower, throw on clothes, and run out the door.

She stopped midstride . . . had she gotten the

receipt from her dresser? She may not need it, but what if she did? She removed the strap from her shoulder, and crash ...the cute little metal, lunchbox-shaped, Wendy Stephens satchel that she'd scored at a sample sale last week hit the sidewalk and popped open. The contents ejected like missiles. Now she was really getting pissed off.

"Damn it!" she hissed, dropping to the ground and picking up her belongings. Thank God she'd only had a few items in it—one being the purple receipt that she grabbed before the wind could pick it up.

"Can I help you?" A woman hovered above her.

The morning sun cast a slight shadow over her face. She raised a hand and squinted for a better view. It was a familiar face, but not one that she knew. Maybe a tenant in her building, but she couldn't be sure.

On her feet again, she replied, "Thanks, I'm good." And then she was on the run again, pulling the car door open and tossing her purse on the seat.

She started the engine and felt a twinge of guilt when she didn't even give it sixty seconds to let the oil rise before putting it in reverse and pulling out of the parking lot. She knew better than to treat the car that way, but this was one time she had to make an exception.

A horn blared behind her as she hastily cut a driver off when she pulled onto the street.

"Sorry," she murmured under her breath while stealing a peek at the offended man in the rearview mirror. Middle finger up, he told her what he thought of her driving. A smile tipped her lip. She was definitely in the wrong for that move, but she couldn't take it back now, and she certainly didn't regret it, particularly when she sailed under a yellow light that surely would have caught her on red had she been more courteous.

For some reason, the woman who had offered to help her came back to mind. She didn't live in the building. She was sure of that now, but she'd seen her around. An uneasiness crept over her, but she dismissed it and pushed the power button for the radio. Music would help with the drive. Music would calm her nerves. The radio emitted a burst of static before the car came to a complete stop. It literally halted in the middle of the street. Horns honked all around her—on the left and the right and from the rear.

"What the hell?" She turned the key to off and put her foot on the gas to start it again.

Prologue

Click, click was the only noise it made. Before she could curse again, the car shook so hard her head hit the steering wheel. The last thing she remembered was a deafening explosion.

1

Linda McNair shrieked, bounced from her chair, and did a happy dance around her desk. She'd gotten the job. She'd gotten the job every freelance fashion photographer in New York City had wanted.

She claimed her seat again, but only because she had to make sure her eyes weren't deceiving her. She'd been feeling duped all day by the insistent barrage of anonymous text messages she'd been receiving. Anxiety about those messages threatened to creep in, but she shrugged it off. She had good news. Good news she'd been waiting for. She reread the message:

Linda,

Your portfolio and references were both impressive. Ross Brothers has decided to go with your studio for the fall print shoot. I'm jumping on a plane, but let's plan to talk first thing Monday morning about the particulars. We're on a tight deadline to get the catalog done, so lace up your roller skates. Have a great weekend, and congrats!

Bo

She let her head drop back and whispered a silent prayer. It wasn't even the end of the January, and her New Year's plan to double her freelance income was already coming to fruition. All she'd had to do was put the word out that she was looking for work, and it was practically falling in her lap. She could hardly believe it.

Linda folded her arms over her chest and leaned back against the cool leather headrest on her chair. Who would have thought shy, introverted, Linda McNair, who grew up in Seattle sheltered by her parents would have this much career success at her age. Twenty-nine was young in any field, but in the world of fashion photography, most artists her age were still looking for their first assistant job with an established photographer. But not her. She'd taken a chance on doing her own thing for a few years after college, then had signed on with *Flaunt Magazine*, and her portfolio had grown and grown.

Her phone beeped to announce a new text message, and she froze. Her heart began to pound in rapid beats, and her arms tensed up. All the joy she'd just been feeling evaporated from her soul. *Not again,* she thought.

Linda was beginning to hate her cell phone and her office phone. Phones were becoming the enemy, but she couldn't ignore them. They were a necessity. She bit her lip and reached for her cell. Relief flooded her when she saw it was a message from her boyfriend, Steve. *Thinking about the day I met you. Best day of my life and it's been the best two years of my life.* An anniversary. This was a first. She'd never been involved with a man for this long in her entire life. But Steve was special. She'd recognized that the first day she met him.

She had stopped in for lunch that afternoon at her favorite carryout restaurant and was flying from the counter to the door in a rush to get back to her studio when she'd run right into another customer.

"Oh my God!" Linda shrieked. She couldn't believe she'd been such a klutz. She looked down at the mess her spilled ice tea had made all over the floor and then let her eyes follow the upward trail to the soaked slacks of the man in front of her. She was horrified. But as her eyes continued their upward path to meet his, the adrenaline shot through her veins. It wasn't just because the man she'd nearly assaulted was so tall and good-looking, or because his skin was sun-kissed and flawlessly tanned like he'd just returned from a vacation to Bora Bora. Nor was it the way his athletic body had felt pressed against hers when she'd slammed against it, or how perfectly his dirty blond hair lay. No. Those attributes, though stunning, weren't the ones that had mesmerized her. It was those piercing, cool blue eyes that had nearly hypnotized her on the spot, and even though their color wasn't warm, they emitted a gentle heat that said he'd forgiven her even before she'd asked. Linda felt winded, but managed to speak her pitiful apology. "I am so sorry."

Their gazes locked for a moment, but when released, she noted his quick once-over of her from head to toe before he smiled and putting his amazingly white teeth on display. *More perfection,* she had thought. Everything about him said 'pulled together'—except, now, for his suit. Thanks to her. She reached into her handbag for her wallet. "Please let me pay for your dry cleaning." She removed a twenty dollar bill.

He raised a hand to hers, curling her fingers around the twenty, and said, "That won't be necessary."

Linda's breath caught at his touch. She dropped her eyes to his fingers, noting that he hadn't let her hand go. Magnetic. That's what this connection was. It scared her. She removed her hand. "I insist," she continued.

One of the restaurant's waitstaff came over with a mop. He looked annoyed that she'd made such a mess, so Linda apologized to him also.

She felt a hand on her elbow. The man she'd soaked from the knees down was pulling her out of the busboy's way. He leaned close to her ear and said, "I'm Steve Mitchell, and you are?"

Linda followed him away from the mess, gently easing her elbow from his grasp. "I'm someone who feels awful for ruining your suit." She held the twenty dollar bill out again and said, "I'll feel horrible if you don't let me compensate you. It's only lunchtime. You'll be terribly uncomfortable all afternoon."

He leaned in again, and this time she caught a whiff of his cologne. A sexy, woodsy scent that she thought might be the new Giorgio Armani fragrance. "I keep a change in the office," he whispered. "A man has to be prepared for pretty women rushing about in this city."

Linda self-consciously licked her lips. "Well, I'm glad you won't be all sticky."

"Sticky, huh?" He flashed those white teeth at her again. "Not today." His voice was flirtatious. "I tell you what. You do owe me, so I was thinking there's something else you can do instead."

Linda cocked her head. He was talking of stickiness and something else she could do for him. She sure hoped his mind had not gone where she thought it had. "Look, I don't know what you have in mind—"

"Lunch," he said, cutting her off. "I had lunch in mind."

Linda's brow knit. He'd surprised her. "I didn't make enough of a mess of your wardrobe? Or do you ask every woman that you bump into to have lunch with you?"

Steve Mitchell chuckled. "Only the ones who take my breath away."

Linda pursed her lips. "Breathless often?" she asked.

Steve shook his head and replied, "Rarely."

She wasn't sure why she'd given him her business card that day. She had thought it was his obscenely good looks, but thinking back now, she realized it was the intensity with which he had released that single word from his lips. *Rarely.* In an instant, she'd felt unique and special. He'd seduced her in less time than it'd taken for that Styrofoam cup to hit the floor, and now, two years later, he was still doing it. He was still taking her breath away.

Linda smiled and sent a text back to him.

Happy Anniversary to you too.

Seconds after she sent it, another message came through. She smiled, thinking how thoughtful he was being today. But then, once she opened it, she swore under her breath. It was Marc, letting her know that he was at the restaurant where they were meeting for dinner.

She hated being late—especially for something with Marc. He was always reminding her that she was the definition of a stereotype. "Losers are on C.P. time," he'd say. And to make her lack of timeliness worse, this was a special night for him. They were celebrating his promotion. She cursed again and pressed a speed dial number. When he answered the call, there was so much noise in the background that she couldn't quite hear him clearly.

"Marc, if you can hear me, I'm running late. See you in a few." She hoped that he heard her.

She pushed her chair back, grabbed her nearby handbag, and rushed toward the door, pulling her coat from the coat rack as she passed it. Before leaving, she turned and looked at the prints that were scattered across the conference room table. She was behind on her deadline to get the photos from the exclusive shoot with Victoria's Lingerie completed early, which meant she'd have to come back after dinner. There was no point in taking the time to shut down the computer. She pulled the door closed behind her and turned the key in the deadbolt.

The spot where they were meeting was within walking distance from her studio. The January wind whirled around, nipping at her face as she exited the building. She tightened her coat around her in an attempt to keep warm, but it wasn't working. She was shivering, and it wasn't just the cold. The street was unusually deserted for a Tuesday evening. Darkness had stolen the sun's rays away, and the dying streetlamp on the corner in front of her made a crackling sound that added to the eeriness.

Linda thought about the text messages and phone calls she'd received. She stopped in her tracks when she thought she heard a noise behind her. Heart slamming in her chest, she turned. No one there. She swallowed and made quick steps down the street to the restaurant. Just as she approached the door, her phone chirped in a text message. She reached into her pocket, thinking it was Marc, and removed her cell to check it.

A sad smiley face.

A violent shiver passed through her entire body. She swallowed. Instinctively, she looked around her and over her shoulder. Was someone following her? She dropped her phone in her bag and closed her eyes for a moment. *This is too much,* she thought. This has been going on for too long to be kids playing as she had originally suspected.

She pulled on the door to the restaurant and stepped inside. Instantly, the lobby's warmth and safety enveloped her. There were people here. Not as many as there usually were, but she spotted the one who would make her feel the safest. Marc was in the far right corner of the restaurant—one hand on a beer and the other on a newspaper, no doubt his favorite, the *Wall Street Journal*.

Linda released a cleansing breath, handed her coat to the coat check attendant, and made her way to the table.

Marc stood, as he always did when she approached the table, and she leaned in and kissed him on his cheek.

"Don't say it," she said.

"I got your call," Marc replied, pulling her chair out. "You're going to be late to your own Photography Masters Cup event."

"Ha, ha," Linda said taking her seat. "I won't be late for that."

"You know we are whatever we do."

"Excellence then is a habit," Linda said, finishing the Aristotle quote he had begun. "I'm only late for personal stuff. I'm never late for business."

"Says you," Marc replied, folding his paper. He stared at her for a moment.

She became self-conscious, looking down at her cherry red dress to see if she'd spilled something on it. But she didn't see anything. "Is there something on my face?" she asked, touching the corners of her mouth.

"Nah, lil sis, you just look kind of pretty tonight."

Linda smirked. "Kind of?"

"Well, you know. As pretty as you can look to me." Marc raised his sweating glass and took a long sip of his beer. "Sometimes you come out of that studio looking like you been in a dark cave instead of dark room."

Linda smirked again and picked up her menu. "All the better to serve our clients—" She stopped midsentence. "Clients! Oh my God . . . congrats on your deal!" She jumped up from her chair and reached over to give Marc a hug.

"I was starting to think you forgot."

Linda reclaimed her chair. Marc's lips spread wide, boasting a smile. "You're a rock star," she said. "I'm so proud of you."

Marc took another sip of his beer and said, "You know how we do it. Work hard, play later."

"I know, but even with working hard, landing *Ouch Magazine* was a big deal."

"Yeah, it was," Marc replied. "Maybe I can get you some work over there."

Linda picked up her menu and let out a long sigh. "That would be great, but sometimes I think I already have more than I can handle."

"You're too meticulous, girl. You need to push some of those photos out faster."

Linda let her shoulders drop. She and Marc had had this conversation before. He was a numbers man. There was no way he could understand that, as a photographer, her work took precision and time. She couldn't cut corners and rush through a program. She wasn't dealing with Excel or Access. She was creating art. "We've had this conversation before." She glanced at the menu and decided on the dish she always had before closing it. "It may be time for me to take on an intern."

"It's past time." Marc frowned. "I've been telling you that.

The waitress approached their table and, after some not so subtle flirting with Marc, took their orders. Marc was by far too good-looking a brother to be in the friend zone. He wasn't exceptionally tall, but he was tall enough for most women. He had great skin which made him look like a velvety smooth chocolate bar and dimples that would make any woman's heart flutter. Women friends were always surprised that he was so good-looking when she introduced him for the first time. They all quickly followed up with the question, "Are you guys dating or something?" Even though they knew about Steve.

"Nothing wrong with having vanilla *and* chocolate ice cream. They have a name for it—the swirl," one of her more brazen colleagues had stated. But Linda had never thought of Marc that way. She had already been involved with Steve when she met him, and Marc's initial approach was all business. He was a consultant, and she needed a new business plan. The fast friendship came as a result of them working together so closely.

Marc's phone rang, rousing her from her thoughts. He looked at it and said, "I have to take this, lil sis." Then he stood and walked away from the table.

Linda found that odd. He took business calls but rarely excused himself. She shrugged it off and pulled her own phone from her bag. She swiped the screen, and the sad smiley appeared again. It had been waiting for her like an omen that refused to go away. She closed the text message, closed her eyes, and dropped her head back. Fingers on her shoulder caused her to nearly jump out of her seat. She bumped the table so hard her water goblet spilled.

Marc hovered above her and then, after

picking up her glass, said, "Damn, girl. You had that look like you needed somebody to work the kinks out of your neck."

Linda picked up a napkin and dabbed at the water puddle on the table. "I'm sorry."

"Why are you so jumpy?"

She shook her head. "I know this is going to sound crazy, but . . . someone is harassing me."

Marc raised an eyebrow. "What do you mean?"

"I mean, I'm getting weird phone calls and text messages. I feel like I'm being followed sometimes. I don't know. Something's going on."

Marc released a long plume of air, his brow knit in a frown. "How long has this been going on?"

"A while."

"A while . . . Like how long, Linda?"

She could see the concern etched on his face. She was grateful for it because it was more than she'd gotten from Steve. He'd dismissed the entire thing as kids playing on the phone and her overactive imagination. *You don't have an enemy on the earth, Linda. Who would follow you?* he'd said, and she'd cosigned to that for a while, but then the calls that had started on the office line began to come in on her cell phone. That wasn't kids. She shared her thoughts about it with Marc.

"So what about the police?" he asked, raising his beer again.

"What do I say? The number that comes up seems to be one of those scrambled numbers like the ones that those annoying telemarketers use, which leaves me with no real number to report. I haven't actually seen anyone following me. It's just a feeling."

Marc nodded.

"I have seen a strange car on my block lately. It drives by slowly and doesn't always park. It seems like it leaves when I come out the door or when I get home. It's weird."

Marc raised his eyebrows. "That part does sound like an overactive imagination. I mean, why would stalker leave when you show up? Don't they usually follow you?"

Linda shook her head. "I don't know how this works. I've never experienced it before. All I know is something is *not* right. I can feel it in my gut."

"Then you should report it." A beat of silence passed between them. "So what does Steve say about it?"

"He thinks I'm being paranoid," she replied, rolling her eyes.

"Is that so?" Marc said. "Typical."

"Don't start, Marc. I love him."

"The question is, does he love you?" Marc deadpanned, and she responded to his comment with the same intense stare.

"Of course he loves me. Why do you always have to question that?"

"Because you're scared as hell. Even I can see that, and your man isn't taking you seriously. That's why. I mean, I don't know about you being followed—a car in the neighborhood could be anything—but the phone calls on both phones is a bit much. Maybe it's a pissed off model or something." Marc finished his drink and picked up his phone. "I just got an email. I need to make a call." He stood again and left the table.

The food was delivered while he was gone. Linda reached for the glass of wine the waitress had delivered for her and nearly downed it in one swig. Her hands shook, and she found herself looking at the door every time it opened. Marc was right. She was afraid.

He returned to the table, and her phone chirped a text. With her free hand, she reached in

16

her bag for the cell. Linda dropped the wineglass when she read the message. Her vision blurred with the tears that instantly filled her eyes.

"Linda," Marc called. "What's wrong?"

She shoved the phone in his direction and watched as he studied it with a frown before reading it out loud. "Bitch, I hope you choke on a snail."

His eyes met her again. This time she could see more than a little concern, and seeing his fear made her entire body shake. "So do you believe I'm being followed now?"

2

The earsplitting sound of Latin music awoke Linda.

"Carmen." She moaned her roommate's name as she flipped over in bed and covered her head with a pillow. Linda's roommate, Carmen, was already up, doing her own version of Zumba.

Linda decided that there was no use staying in bed with the sound of loud music bouncing off the walls. She rolled her eyes and sucked her teeth then slid out of bed and headed for the shower. She had planned to drive into Manhattan today instead of taking the subway. She wanted to see if any of the photos from the spring swimwear shoot she had photographed a few days ago needed post-processing. She hated to do photo clean ups, much preferring to get the shot correct in the camera because the cleanup work was time consuming.

When she stepped out of the shower, she was able to hear the sound of her cell phone ringtone blaring Beyoncé's "Put a Ring on it" over the loud music penetrating through walls. The ringtone was compliments of Carmen. She'd set it one day when she asked to borrow Linda's phone while hers was charging. Dripping wet, Linda pulled a towel from the wall rack, wrapped it around herself, and rushed to the dresser where she had laid the phone down. There was no name registering in the caller ID, but she pressed the answer button anyway since she had the phone in her hand.

She tried to catch her breath. "Hello." There was no response from the other end, but she sensed that the caller was still present.

"Hello," she repeated, "I know you're there. Who is this?" she asked, stiffly annoyed that the person wasn't responding. She held the phone to her ear for a few seconds more before she heard a click. The caller had hung up. Linda looked up into the air and exhaled sharply. She wondered who kept calling her and why she was their target. She was so sick of these calls.

She'd already mentally ticked through a list of people she knew, trying to think of anyone who might dislike her enough to torture her like this, but no one came to mind. Not really. She didn't have enemies. But the calls were concerning because she realized they'd began around the same time she started having the feeling she was being followed.

By the time she had dressed, Carmen's music had stopped. Her roommate was dressed in her workout gear—spandex capris and a sports bra—and was seated at the end of the kitchen island, sipping orange juice from a glass when Linda entered.

"Hola, Linda," Carmen said in a bubbly voice as Linda made her way to the refrigerator and opened the door, taking out some fruits and veggies for the juicer.

"Girl, don't *hola* me." Linda peered around the refrigerator door at Carmen.

"Hey, what's wrong? What did the guy do now?" Carmen grimaced.

"Not him, you." Linda smirked.

"What you mean me? What did I do?" Carmen feigned innocence.

Linda raised an eyebrow. "I had planned on

sleeping in today until I was Zumba-ed out of my sleep."

"Oh. That." Carmen shrugged. "I'm sorry. I didn't know you were still here. You're usually already up and gone by now." Carmen walked over and put her empty glass in the sink. "If I'd known you were still sleeping, I would've turned it down a decibel or two. Maybe." She wiggled her eyebrows.

"Yeah, right." Linda side-eyed her. "Why do you turn up the stereo so loud anyway? Enough to wake the whole city."

"Girl, you gotta feel the music. You can't get your dance on when it's too low. You know what I mean?" Carmen swayed her hips from side to side, snapping her fingers.

Linda shook her head. "Yeah, keep it up and the neighbors are gonna make sure that we're dancing our way to a new home."

"Alright. I get the message . . . I promise I'll try to do better."

She turned to Linda and asked, "By the way, could I borrow your car on Wednesday? I need to go over to Brooklyn to pick up the dance costumes for my troupe."

Linda gave the question some thought before answering. She wasn't happy that each time

Carmen borrowed her car, a new dent appeared. "Let me think about that one for a moment."

"You know how crazy these people park around here. I leave enough space, but somehow they seem to be attracted to your car like a magnet."

"So how come I can come away without a dent?"

"I don't know. I try to be really careful, but these nut jobs get too close. C'mon. I promise to be extra careful." Carmen clasped her hands together and pleaded teasingly.

"You're lucky I'm not all that particular about the exterior because it's not brand spanking new." Linda scooped a spoonful of the juice she'd just made and dipped her tongue in it, swirling it around in her mouth.

"Thank you! When are you going to come to one of my shows, chica?" she asked, eyeing Linda closely.

"When's your next one?"

"In three weeks. We're putting on a show at a small theatre in Brooklyn. It's going to be fantastic!" Carmen said, dancing in place.

Linda laughed haughtily as she poured the rest of the blended juice into a tall plastic container to carry with her to her studio office. She turned back to Carmen. "I almost forgot to ask. How did your date go last night?"

Carmen sucked her teeth and rolled her eyes. "Humph . . . If that's what you wanna call it."

Linda cocked her head. "What happened?"

"Well first off, his idea of a date was meeting up at Mario's."

"And what's wrong with Mario's? It's a nice restaurant." Linda wiped the overflowed juice from the side of container. "I've eaten there before. The food is great."

Carmen waited a beat. "Mario's *Pizza*. That little place on the corner of Fulton."

Linda bit her lip, trying to hide the smile that was fighting to escape. Her roommate was petite, but a force to be reckoned with. She could only imagine what had gone down in that pizza parlor.

Carmen poured a cup of tea and reclaimed her seat at the island. She blew on the steaming liquid before taking a cautious sip. "It was a total disaster." She brushed back her curly black, shoulder-length hair.

"And if being cheap wasn't enough, we stood eye to eye. He couldn't have been more than a half inch taller," she muttered.

"C'mon. Really? You never give these guys a chance. Maybe he wanted to do one of those meet and greet things to see if there was chemistry."

"Easy for you to say. You got some well-to-do hot shot." She lifted her cup to take another sip but changed her mind and put it down. "I don't know why I let you talk me into online d—"

"You know I'm not with Steve for his money," Linda cut her off and shot her an annoyed look.

"Lighten up. I know that." Carmen took her half empty cup and placed it in the sink. Turning to face Linda, she crossed her arms in front of her and added, "I'm done with men for a while. I don't trust them anyway. They're either cheap or they're cheats."

***

The hairs on Linda's neck stood up. She glanced in her rearview mirror and noticed a car had been trailing her since she pulled out of the parking lot fifteen minutes ago. She pressed her foot down on the gas pedal in an attempt to accelerate, but the car barely increased in speed. "Damn." She made a mental note to get that checked. She veered off the main road into a Trader Joe's parking lot. She thought if someone was really following her, she'd know for sure if they turned, too. She looked into her rearview mirror and saw the dark blue Honda still behind her. Her heart started racing. She wasn't being paranoid after all. Someone really was following her. She reached for her cell phone on the console, not quite sure who to call. She glanced up again in the mirror to see if she could see the license plate number. At least she'd have something to give to the police. But before she could get it, the car sped off. She looked as it passed to see if she could see the driver, but the windows were tinted too dark.

Linda was shaking so badly her hands could barely grip the steering wheel. She couldn't drive, so she stopped and sat in her car for a few minutes to try to pull herself together. She had never been afraid of anything, but this made her feel so vulnerable. She thought of calling the police anyway, but she had nothing concrete to report. She picked up her phone and speed-dialed Steve. Talking to him would calm her nerves. His voicemail message came on, and she decided against leaving him a message. She would tell him when she saw him. She put the phone back down and leaned her head back against the seat, closing her eyes and taking a deep breath. "Dear God, what is going on?" she asked herself out loud.

Linda almost jumped out of her skin when she heard loud tapping against the car window.

"Miss? Are you okay?" asked an elderly woman wearing a bright red knit hat and matching scarf tied around her neck. Linda pressed the button that rolled the car window down and immediately felt the cold air splash her face.

"Yes, I'm fine," she muttered, offering a small smile.

"Then why are you sitting there in your car blocking parking spaces? I thought you might be dead or something." She smirked. "Can you move your car so I can park?"

Shivering from the cold air filtering into the car, Linda let up the window. She shifted into drive and proceeded to drive away. Just then, her cell phone rang. She reached down and picked it up. Still somewhat shaken from the ordeal, she spoke into the phone in quiet greeting. At first, there was no response. Then she heard a muffled laugh. She couldn't tell if it was a man or a woman.

"Who are you?" she shouted at the phone. No response. The phone was silent until she heard the click of the caller disconnecting.

3

Linda lost track of time as she dove into her work, cleaning up and organizing the photos from the photo shoot earlier in the week. Her love for taking pictures as a child had developed into a photography career which had, in turn, led her to working with one of New York's top fashion magazines. She had turned off her cell phone because she didn't want to be distracted—and also because she just couldn't bear another creepy call like the one she had received earlier. She was startled by a knock at the door. She wasn't expecting anyone, and she never had clients just show up. Her heart dropped to her stomach. What if it was the creep that had been following her earlier? She reached for her purse and took out the keychain unit of pepper spray that Marc had given her. She had only thrown it in her purse to appease him, with no real intention of keeping it, but now she was glad that she had. She pressed the button to turn her cell phone back on in case she needed to call for help, then she walked over to the door.

"Who's there?" she yelled through the door, using the firmest and most controlled tone she could manage.

"It's me, babe."

She breathed a sigh of relief and unlocked the door.

Usually, she was glad to see him at her door because he always looked so devilishly handsome—his sparkling blue eyes and pearly white teeth would be a welcome sight at any woman's door. But today it was his company she was happy for. She fell against him and gave him a tight hug.

"Why are you so surprised to see me? We made a date for today." He kissed her on the forehead, and they entered the studio.

"I'd almost forgot about it. I've been distracted."

"I texted you before coming over," he added.

"My phone was off. I was trying to get some work done without interruptions."

Steve looked down, and Linda realized she still held her weapon. "What is that?" he asked.

She looked down at her hand and replied, "Pepper spray."

"Okay, so I get it a woman can't be too safe in this city, but why in the world did you answer the door holding pepper spray?"

"Remember I told you someone has been following me?"

He sighed like he didn't quite want to hear about it again, and then he nodded.

"Well, today when I got into my car, I was being followed. At first, I thought that maybe I was just being a bit paranoid, so I quickly turned off the highway and into a supermarket parking lot, and the car behind me pulled in right behind me. I was so scared."

He placed his hands on her shoulders and chuckled. "Honey, that person could have actually been going to the supermarket. Why do you think you were being followed?"

She pulled out of his embrace. "Why can't you take me seriously about this? Have I ever in the entire two years that we've been dating been irrational?"

"Babe, I do take you seriously. I just think that you can be a little melodramatic at times."

His tone had quickly become condescending, and she was regretting that she had agreed to go the film festival.

She walked back over to her work station. He followed behind her, closing the distance and enveloping her in his arms. He trailed feather-soft kisses down her neck and then whispered against her skin, "I've had a crazy morning. I'm sorry, but the drama at my office is about all the drama I can take for today."

Linda turned to face him. She could see the stress of the day in his eyes, and she felt genuinely bad for him. "What happened?"

He shook his head. "I don't want to talk about it. You know what I really want? I want to make love to you right here on this desk."

Linda felt his hardness growing against her as he flexed his hips forward, sending a shiver through her body. She wanted nothing more than for Steve to take her—right there and then—but her disappointment over him not believing her was overshadowing her desire. And her resentment about not being privy to his entire life had dampened her sexual appetite as well. She loosened his hold on her and stepped away, her eyes filling with tears. In her peripheral vision, she could see him wiping his face with his hand in frustration.

"What's wrong?" he asked.

Her cell phone rang while it was still in her hand. She checked the caller ID and saw it was Marc. She hesitated for a moment, but then decided to answer it.

"Hi, Marc." She tried to sound cheerful but was failing miserably.

"What's wrong, lil sis? You sound down. Need me to come over?"

"I'm fine. No, that won't be necessary." She was grateful for the comforting support that Marc provided as a friend and wished that he was there. She thought he would make a good boyfriend and wondered why he didn't have a girlfriend. She had often wondered if maybe he was gay because she just could not understand why a brother as fine as Marc wasn't involved in some kind of intimate relationship.

"I need to stop by anyway. I have to give

you the details about that Stein & Bradley clothing account."

Steve cleared his throat, signaling Linda that he was growing impatient.

"Listen, Marc, I have to go. I'll call you later." She spoke softly into the phone, "I said that I was fine. Steve's here with me." She looked in Steve's direction.

"No wonder you sound so sad. What has that punk done now?" Marc's voice became angry over the phone.

"Ciao, Marc." Linda couldn't help but grin as she pictured his frown. She couldn't understand why Marc disliked Steve so much. They had only met once or twice and even then hadn't been in each other's presence for that long.

When she looked up at the end of her call, Steve was standing closer to her, a frown on his face.

"Why is that guy always calling you and hanging around?"

"Don't go there. Marc is just a very good friend." Linda rolled her eyes.

"I'm not sure he feels the same way. I've seen the way he looks at you."

Linda scowled. "Really? Exactly how many times

have you seen him? And you've already gathered from that he has a thing for me? Please."

She picked up one of her photos, examining it closely.

"I've got a special evening planned, and you need to go home and change for it," he said.

She cast a glance at his attire. He always looked nice, but the suit he was wearing was not something he'd wear for anything other than work.

As if he'd read her mind, he said, "I have a change of clothes in the car."

Linda put away the photos she had been working on. Steve helped her into her coat. He turned her to face him and pulled her close, kissing her softly on the lips. She parted her lips, and he slid his tongue into her mouth, deepening the kiss. She allowed him to explore every inch of her mouth with his tongue. Her body began to respond to his kiss. Her head was starting to spin. She could feel the wanton urgency growing inside her. Just then, Steve ended the kiss and took a step back. "We'd better go now before we don't make it there at all." He grinned.

Linda caught her breath. No matter how much of a jerk Steve had been earlier, she loved him deeply and yearned for his touch. As much as she wanted to see the movie, she wanted him to make love to her right there.

"Do we really have to go?" she asked in her sexiest voice, hoping to seduce him into staying.

He studied her for a moment with his brow raised. "Yes, we do. We've been waiting to see this movie for a long time, and tonight is the last night it's showing."

She pouted before grabbing the keys from her desk and handing them to him to lock the door behind them. They were on their way to the Lincoln Center for a film festival.

4

Dinner at the Grand Tier Restaurant in Lincoln Center made up for the anger she'd been feeling towards Steve. He'd arranged an open table reservation, which she found to be extremely thoughtful. Linda had to remind herself that aside from his not taking her seriously about the stalker, Steve had always been the best boyfriend a woman could ever ask for. He was attentive, generous, and he had everything going for him career-wise. Marriage wasn't necessarily on her agenda, but if she was going to be exclusive in a relationship, the man needed to be someone worth being exclusive for.

"I got something for you," Steve whispered.

His warm breath against her neck sent an electrifying thrill down her spine.

She stopped walking and turned to face him, wishing now she'd let him make love to her earlier so she wouldn't be wanting him all through dinner.

"We said no gifts," she stated leaning into him.

"I couldn't help it," Steve replied. "Every time I look at you I want to give you something."

Linda laughed. That line was a joke between them. Early on in their relationship, Steve had brought her a gift of some kind every time they had a date. When Linda asked why he did it, his response was "I don't know. Every time I see you I want to give you something." He even whispered it in her ear some nights when they were making love. It was one of the sweetest and sexiest things he had ever said to her.

"I followed the rules. I didn't get you anything, and now I'm going to feel bad," Linda pouted.

"Never feel badly. Having you on my arm is gift enough," he replied.

They strolled some of the shops in Lincoln Center before heading to the theater where the

"Wild West Classics" were showing. She and Steve loved westerns. He insisted all men did, but for her, they took her back to those childhood days with her father. Westerns had dominated the family room television, and Linda found herself watching just so she could get quality time with her dad. Now she equated them to modern day urban films where men fought over territory and women—everybody showing up at the club strapped, fights breaking out at the bar, the sheriff aka da PoPo shutting everything down, women pimping themselves to form alliances with the powerhouses, wars over gold the same as drug wars. In her opinion, westerns were the original gangsta flicks.

Steve and she were enjoying the movie when she felt her phone buzzing loudly inside her purse. She reached for it to place it on silent, but looked at the screen out of curiosity to see who was calling. She could see she had a message, so she decided to put the phone away and made a mental note to check her messages as soon as she exited the theater.

Linda tucked the phone back and snuggled up against Steve, inhaling his cologne which had a spicy musk that smelled a bit like vanilla. He immediately slid his arm around her and kissed her softly on her forehead.

When the movie ended, Linda wasted no time digging into her purse to retrieve her phone, anxious to find out who had left a message. She ran her fingers mechanically over the phone, touching buttons while walking out of the theater and almost tripping over a tear in the worn carpet.

"Babe, can't that wait until later?" Steve grimaced.

"You know I have no patience. I've been expecting a call from a potential client on the West Coast." She glanced up at Steve then shifted her eyes back to her phone, tapping in her pass code a second time to unlock the phone. She found it to be a pain in the butt to put in a code each time her phone screen locked, but she knew it was necessary to protect her privacy. She had already lost a phone twice.

Steve held her elbow, lightly guiding her out of the way of the other patrons pouring out of the theater and to a near empty area where she could check her messages. She bypassed the messages from Carmen and her mother and waited for the third one to play. There was silence at first, and then a muffled, hoarse voice said, "Hope you enjoyed the movie. It'll soon be your last, bitch." It ended with that horrid laugh again—the one she'd heard that day in the parking lot. Her eyes widened, and her hands begin to tremble as she pressed the button to end her messages. She felt the tiny hairs on the nape of her neck stand at attention. She quickly scanned the movie theater, turning her head from left to right, wondering if the caller was watching her as she listened to the message. She looked up at Steve, her face frozen glazed over in horror.

"Baby, what's wrong?" Steve pulled her close to him, his hands resting at her waist. He raised one hand and cupped her face. "You look as though you've seen a ghost. Is everything okay? Who was that? Tell me what's wrong."

Linda stared out into space for a few moments before she was able to speak. She had to admit to herself that this last phone call had really crippled her with fright. She swallowed hard before speaking, her voice and her body shaking. "It was my stalker," she said in a low, trembling voice a few decibels above a library whisper.

5

Steve held the door to his apartment open to allowed Linda to walk in ahead of him. He unbuttoned her coat, pulled it from her shoulders, and she slid her arms out. She hadn't talked much in the car on the way over, still shaken by that disturbing call she had received from the stalker. Steve had followed her to her apartment first to drop off her car so that Carmen would have it for her trip to Brooklyn.

"Can I get you something, baby?" he asked. He didn't give her a chance to respond. "You need a glass of wine." He took quick steps to the bar, and she watched as he opened a bottle.

Linda realized she'd been transfixed in the

same position since he'd left. She took a seat on the plush leather couch. Her eyes roamed the large and spacious room. Although elegant, it had a masculine décor with furnishings and paintings from various places around the world. The earth-tone walls contrasted sharply with the white carpet. The warmth of the room was inviting, taking off the winter chill. A hint of lemon and lavender lingered in the air. She suspected that the housekeeper had just cleaned. He poured wine into two glasses and handed one to her. She took the glass and brought it to her lips, swallowing it all one big gulp before lowering it to the glass-top coffee table.

"I'm worried about you." He smoothed back a tendril of her hair and tucked it behind her ear. "How long has this been going on? Calls like the one you received today?"

When did they start? she mused. "I'm not really sure—a few months ago, maybe. I didn't pay them too much attention at first because I thought that they were just prank calls or kids playing games as you had suggested. But then over the past few weeks, they've increased in frequency—and the messages got nastier. Plus, I told you I've been feeling like someone is following me." She fell back against the chair.

"Do you have any idea who this person could be? I mean, could it be someone that you work with?"

"I don't know. As a photographer, I meet so many different people while on assignment. But I don't have any enemies. I go out of my way to be nice to people. And I'm always professional."

"Think, Linda. There has to be something. Maybe even someone disgruntled about a bill," he continued. "If they have access to your work line and cell, it may be connected to work."

"My cell is on my business cards," she said. "I give those to everybody, not just people having to do with work."

"But everybody isn't going to follow you," he added.

Linda sighed, reaching for his untouched glass of wine, swallowing it down rather quickly. She was glad he was taking her seriously on this matter, but still annoyed that her life had to be threatened in order for him to do so.

"You're going to have to report this to the police. Not that I'm trying to scare you—but I don't think it's going to stop. It seems as though you've been putting up with these calls and dismissing them as if they were insignificant—but this is serious."

"I don't have enough evidence to let the police in on this yet." She looked away from his gaze, thinking she could certainly do without being dragged through the coals by the police. They always seemed to turn these things around to make the victim look like she'd asked for it to happen to her.

He took her hand and sandwiched it in between his. "Babe, you don't need any evidence. Just tell them that someone has been following you. Just the phone calls should be enough."

"I don't think so. What if they ask me questions about what he looks like? I don't have an answer to that. Every time he calls, it's a different number. It's never the same one twice. It's like it's scrambled or something. I don't want to look like some sort of raving lunatic. You know how the police have a way of turning things like this around trying to—"

He interjected, "I would think that you'd want the police to know. Why wouldn't you? Is there something you're not telling me?"

"No, I'm just . . . I don't know." Tears welled up in her eyes then came trickling down her cheeks, and she broke out into uncontrollable sobs.

"Come here, baby. Shhh ... it's going to be okay," he said quietly as he wound his arm around her and pulled her tighter against him. She was a mass of conflicting emotions as she pressed against his chest. The smell of his masculinity filled her nostrils, and the thud of his racing heart sent a burning desire through her. He bent his head, lowering his mouth onto hers. The feel of his warm lips touching hers made her quiver. She wanted more of him. She needed him. She parted her lips, greedily accepting his tongue as it slid sensually through, tangling with hers and deepening the kiss.

He broke their kiss long enough to scoop her up into his strong arms and carry her down the short hall into his bedroom. He gently lay her down on the bed. As he stripped off his clothing, her eyes lingered on his manhood as he moved closer to the bed and lay beside her. Their eyes locked as he unbuttoned her blouse and removed it. A soft moan escaped her lips when he circled his finger around the nipple of one bare breast, tugging at it before wrapping his mouth around it and tenderly nibbling and sucking before turning to the other, giving it equal attention. She was falling apart at the seams. He moved back up to her mouth, their kisses more inflamed and their breathing more erratic. Her body ached with wanting him. He briefly broke the kiss to peel the rest of her clothing off. He lavished her body in feathery kisses before settling between her legs, gently parting them and nuzzling her clit with a few light teasing licks before dipping his tongue in deeper and sending her into utter ecstasy.

"Steve!" her voice a strangled cry as she clutched the sheets.

He slid himself up her body and entered her with one quick thrust. "I love you," he whispered.

Hearing his declaration of love to her, words that he scarcely used, brought tears to her eyes. She wrapped her legs around him and arched her back to draw him deeper inside. He quickened his pace, deepening his strokes, increasing the pleasure, taking her to an even higher level of ecstasy and sending sparks of electricity rippling through her body. He tipped his head back and moaned loudly as he spilled into her. Planting his head between her neck and shoulder, he kissed her neck softly before rolling off to rest beside her.

Lying on his side, he propped himself on one

elbow and studied her while the pads of his fingers traced the outline of her lips.

"You're beautiful," he murmured with a crooked grin.

She closed her eyes for a moment, wishing that their time together as they were at that very moment would never end.

"Tell me something." He laid his head back on the pillow, looking up at the ceiling for a moment and then returning his eyes back to her. He reached for her hand and laced his long fingers between hers. "How did I deserve someone as beautiful and as smart as you?"

She shrugged her shoulders, a playful smirk on her lips. "I don't know. Why don't you tell me?"

He nudged her. "You can't answer a question with a question."

They both laughed.

She raised her head, took his arm and looped it around her shoulder, and lay against his chest. "You know, I wish we could be this way more often."

"You mean having sex? I'm all for it." He chuckled.

She pinched him in his side lightly. "No silly, I mean just lie in bed like this, holding each other."

She sprang upright looking down at him holding some loose tresses away from her face. "I know! We can plan a vacation. Let's go to an island where we can relax and—"

"Babe, you know I can't get away right now. There're some major changes being made in the company, and I have to be here—"

She rolled her eyes, sucked her teeth and laid back down. "That's the problem—you never seem to have time for me. For us."

He pulled her back against him. "Hey—where's all this coming from?"

Her voice cracked, "I feel like I had to struggle to get people's acceptance my whole life." "Wait—hold on—what are you talking about now?" He lifted her chin, wiped away a few tears that had rolled down her cheeks. He held her tightly while she shuddered and sobbed against him. She felt internally drained. Her emotions were running high.

She stopped sobbing and swallowed hard against the knot that had developed in her throat. "I never told you this, but growing up, I felt like I was never accepted by the people around me. I've always felt like an outsider because of the way that I looked."

Steve's eyebrows knitted. "What do you mean? You're beautiful."

"It's not easy growing up biracial." She let that statement hang between them and waited for his response. This was the first time that she had actually verbalized her ethnicity to him because she had been unsure of whether or not he would reject her. Not that she was trying to pass for being Caucasian, but she'd been down the road too many times—the one where she was too light for some or not light enough for others. Steve had been different about what she considered to be "her look". Most men she dated asked her right up front—"*What are you?*" Like she was a breed of animal or something. But not Steve. He hadn't been inquisitive at all. He'd never even asked. She wasn't sure if he'd been waiting for her to tell him without him having to ask or if he just didn't care one way or the other.

Just when she thought he wasn't going to respond at all, she felt his body stiffen. "What is it? Something wrong?" she asked.

"No, nothing's wrong. Why would you ask?" His expression gave nothing away.

"You haven't responded to my statement about being biracial, but your body language is speaking volumes. Do you have a problem with it?" she questioned. "If I had told you my father is black, it would have made a difference? Well, what the hell did you think I was?"

"I don't—I guess I just never thought about it. You had plenty of opportunities to tell me. I mean, I've teased you before about being Italian or something because you're always tan, and when I saw that picture of your mother, I just assumed that you were—"

"Caucasian? You assumed I was white because my mother is white? Take another good look at my skin." She stretched her arm out over his. "Do I look—?"

He raked his fingers through his thick blond hair. "You know me better than that. I could care less what color you are. What I'm trying to figure out is why you felt it necessary to keep your ethnicity from me until now? I never asked you because it really didn't matter to me—then or now."

"Then how come you're getting so upset?" She sat up to face him, holding the sheet against her chest.

"I'm not upset. I just think you're making more out of this than what it is. I love you for who you are." He sat upright next to her and caressed her arm. "It doesn't matter to me. I was a little surprised by it, but it doesn't change how I feel about you." He kissed her shoulder. "C'mon. Lie back down and finish telling me about what happened to you growing up. I want to know."

She bit her lip, measuring her next word. After a beat, she cleared her throat. "Well . . . let's see. I—"

6

Steve

"Hold that thought." He pushed himself up, slid off the bed, and pulled on his silk boxers. "I'm going to get that bottle of wine so that we can finish it here."

When he returned with the bottle of wine and glasses, Linda was sitting up in bed with the sheet draped across her. He loved seeing her like that. She was beautiful and relaxed. The vulnerability of her nakedness made him want her again. But he restrained himself. She wanted to talk, and he needed to listen.

He poured more wine into the glasses and handed her one as he sat on the covers next to her.

"So go on—finish telling me." He coaxed her. He smiled and leaned in to plant a kiss on her lips.

She held the glass up to her mouth and drew in a long sip before lowering it to her lap. "Well, there's not much to tell. Basically, I grew up with low self-esteem because, like I said before, I didn't fit in. We lived in a predominantly black neighborhood. The school that I attended was mostly black with a few Latinos and very few whites. I had a natural tendency to identify more with the black kids, but there were times when I wasn't black enough for them. I guess you might say that I went through an identity crisis, not knowing which side of the fence I fit in on. My maternal grandparents would have nothing to do with me because, from what my mother says, they were racists. I never knew my biological father or his parents because he never came around." She raised the glass to her mouth, taking another sip. "We didn't have a lot of money. In fact, my mom worked two jobs to keep up with paying the bills. She was a single mother for a while until she met my stepfather, who also happens to be black." She glanced up at him. "I guess she prefers black men."

"What about you? What do you prefer?" He smiled when he asked, fully expecting her to say white men because, after all, she was here with him. But the question was intended to lighten the mood.

She rewarded him with a coy smile before saying, "I don't know that I have a preference. I have so little experience, it's hard to say." She paused and took another sip.

Steve took in her long slender fingers, swanlike neck, and cover model face. It was hard to imagine that a woman so beautiful could have little experience with men. He'd been mesmerized at first sight.

Linda continued. "One of her two jobs was ..." She hesitated, lowering her eyes to her near empty glass. She was concentrating on it too hard and too long. The words she wanted to say were painful.

He sensed it and gave her time, and then when he thought she'd never get the courage, he prompted. "Go on and finish what you were going to say."

With her eyes still fixed on the glass in her hand, she said, "She was a stripper until she met my stepfather." She continued, "I didn't understand what she did until I was bullied in school. The kids called my mother a whore." She blinked back tears and went on. "I didn't have many friends growing up. I was afraid that friendships wouldn't last once they found out about my mom, so I kept mostly to myself."

A sudden coldness hit his core. Growing up hadn't been easy for her. His heart broke for her. He'd had plenty of friends growing up. He'd been considered one of the cool kids and referred to as the class clown, which got him into trouble a few times. He took comfort in knowing that his mother would be home when he arrived from school. She'd have snacks laid out for him. Baked cookies or fruit. He'd inhale the aroma of freshly baked chocolate chip cookies as soon as he entered the house. He bent forward, brushing a light kiss over her shoulder. "I'm so sorry that life wasn't kind to you growing up."

"Hey, no more sob stories," she said, feigning a smile and wiping her eyes. "So tell me more about *you*, Mr. Mitchell. What was your childhood like?"

"Me?"

"Yes, you." she poked her index finger into his muscular stomach.

"Hmmm. My life was just regular. Nothing much went on."

"I know you can do better than that." She grinned.

"Really. There's not much to tell. Let's see. I grew up in a middle-class family in Brooklyn. I'm an only child—I had an older brother, but he died before I was born. I learned from my parents that he died of pneumonia."

"Really? I'm sorry. You never mentioned a sibling before."

"Yeah. My brother was autistic. My parents have come to believe it was due to a vaccination he received." His expression became solemn.

"Wow. That must've been tough on them. I couldn't imagine losing a child." She caressed his arm.

"Yeah," he said absently.

"Were they overly protective of you?"

"Surprisingly, they didn't smother me or shelter me as you would think they would've. I pretty much had a great childhood with lots of friends," he said.

"You must have been the popular boy in school, huh?" she teased.

"What makes you think that?"

"Because." She smiled.

"Because what?" He pinched her butt, making her squeal.

"Stop that." She giggled.

"So why would you think that I was popular in school? I'm curious."

"Look at you. You know that you're a hottie. Must've had all the girls drooling all over you."

He laughed heartily. "There's only one girl that I'm interested in having drool over me."

"Really?" she responded with a raised eyebrow.

"Yes, really." His hand curved around the nape of her neck and pulled her head closer. He covered her mouth with his, parting her lips with his tongue and exploring the caverns of her mouth.

In moments like this, he wanted to forget that dark cloud hanging over him. He knew it was wrong to keep the truth from Linda, especially since she'd just been forthcoming with him. But he didn't want to lose her. He had to keep that part of his life a secret until he could find a way to fix it.

7

Steve's eyes were beginning to tire from skimming through pages of the quarterly budget report. Although the board meeting wasn't until Monday, he wanted to get a start on reviewing the report so that changes could be made before the meeting. He rubbed his eyes then rested his head back against the top of the leather chair in his home office. He leaned over to pull the desk drawer open, took out a cigar box, and set it on top of the desk. He ran his fingers lightly across the top of the box, feeling the smooth wood surface beneath his fingertips. The Nicaraguan cigars were a gift to him from a client in celebration of closing a very profitable business deal. He didn't smoke cigars often, but at times like this when his mind was cluttered with so many things, he'd indulge to help him to relax and focus.

He released the small metal clasp that secured the box, lifted the top, extracted a torpedo, and held it under his nose, sniffing along its length. He placed the cigar on the desk then pushed his chair out and stood, sauntering over to the matching cherry credenza behind him. He stooped down, opened the door, and withdrew a bottle of scotch whiskey. Combing through a stack of CD's on the shelf above, he pulled out *King of Blue* by jazz artist Miles Davis and slid it into the Bose CD player, selecting one of his favorite tracks, "*Blue in Green.*" He lifted a glass from the tray on top of the credenza and carried both the scotch and the glass to his desk. After filling the glass halfway, he searched through the desk drawer, retrieving the cigar lighter and guillotine. He cut the head of the cigar with one quick chop then lit it and took a puff, savoring the spicy flavors and being mindful not to inhale the smoke. He raised the glass of scotch to his lips and took a sip, its sweet, smoky vanilla flavor mingling with the spicy stogie. He stood up, cigar in one hand and glass of scotch in the other, and walked around the large half-circle desk to the elongated windows to take in the spectacular view of Central Park. He gazed pensively out the window. He could see the Wollman Rink from his window. There were several adults and children gliding across the ice-covered skating rink. He remembered how he and Miriam used to love going over to the rink to ice skate, indulging in a cup of hot cocoa with marshmallows afterwards. He took another puff of the cigar followed by a sip of scotch. His mind wandered back to when he first met Miriam.

Miriam was an honor student in high school, and Steve had to admit he'd never even noticed her until he found out he was failing chemistry and the threat of being benched during football games loomed as a threat. His coach and Mr. Wyant, the chemistry teacher, had suggested that Steve talk to Miriam about tutoring him a few days a week in order to bring his grade up. Initially, Steve was hesitant about asking for help, but playing football and being on the football team was really important to him, and he also liked the fringe benefits of being a jock and having beautiful girls vying for his attention. So it didn't take long for him to approach her—he had too much to lose. She was tall and slender. A red-headed, freckle-faced girl with blue-green eyes. He didn't find her attractive at the start, but she grew on him. She peered up at him briefly and returned to putting her things in her knapsack without speaking a word.

Steve cleared his throat. "Miriam, right?"

Miriam didn't look at him. She stood, zipped her bag, and tossed it over her shoulder. Her action stated loud and clear that she was not impressed as the other girls he approached. She began to walk towards the door leading out of the classroom. Steve rushed to catch up with her.

"Hey. Miriam. Wait a minute!" Steve called out.

Miriam slowed her pace and turned towards him, glaring. "What do you want?"

"What's the mean look for? I just wanna ask you something." Steve raised an eyebrow.

"I know your type. Don't get me mixed up with the fools that drool over you," she warned.

"I promise you, it's nothing like that." Steve tried to sound reassuring. "I was wondering if you had time to tutor me in chemistry. Mr. Wyant suggested to me that you would be the perfect choice." He flashed a bright grin and hoped he hadn't overdone it with the words 'perfect choice.'

Miriam studied him for a moment, not sure whether or not to believe him. "Let me ask you a question, Steve. Do you want to be tutored so that you can keep your position on the football team, or is because you want to learn chemistry?"

Steve hadn't bargained for being judged by a plain Jane—and just to get tutored. This was the first time that he had felt at a loss for words with a girl. He could normally charm his way out of any situation, but he had a feeling it wasn't going to work with Miriam. If he lied, she would see right through him.

Miriam folded her arms across her chest. "I thought so. Listen, jock, don't waste my time."

Steve raised the glass and tossed back the remaining scotch. Satisfied, he returned to his desk. He set the glass down and laid remains of the cigar in an ashtray, letting it burn out freely. His mind was made up. It was time for him to move forward with his plan.

8

She was on edge. Every little noise had her nearly jumping out of her skin.

Like the sound of keys jingling at the door. It sent a wave of terror through her. She made a few steps towards the door but was paralyzed with fear when the door to the apartment squeaked open. Carmen shrieked, which made Linda scream out as well. Even though her rational mind knew that Carmen would be coming home at some point, her nerves had taken over, negating all normal thought.

"What the hell?" Carmen said as she held her hand over her chest, her heart pounding.

"Don't scare me like that," she added, taking a deep breath.

"I'm sorry. I didn't mean to scare you. My nerves got the best of me. I wasn't expecting you home so soon."

"Hello— mi Amiga— I live here. Who else would be coming through the door? By the way, what are you doing home anyway? I thought that you were out with *Mr. Wonderful?*" She removed her hat and coat and hung them both in the hall closet.

"I was out. We went to see one of those old western films then we went back to his place," Linda responded.

Carmen took a few steps closer to Linda. "Then why aren't you still with him?" She rested her hands on her hips, looking up at Linda who stood a few inches taller.

"It's a long story, and I don't want to talk about it right now," Linda mumbled, shifting her eyes to the floor.

"Listen, Linda, something is obviously bothering you. Why don't you tell me what's going on? I know you love this guy, but I don't know, you seem to be stressed a lot lately. Come, I'll put on some coffee and cut us a slice of banana bread, and we can talk about it, yes?" Without waiting for Linda to answer, Carmen swept past her and into the kitchen. She washed her hands and set up the Keurig coffeemaker. A few moments later, the aroma of Green Mountain Coffee Dark Magic spilled into the room. Linda opened the cabinet doors and grabbed two small plates, placing them on the kitchen island next to the loaf of banana bread. Normally she wouldn't have indulged because sweets was her enemy when it came to controlling her weight, but she couldn't resist the smell of that banana bread permeating the air and wafting up her nose. Carmen could afford such indulgences because she worked off calories through her dancing every day.

Carmen filled two mugs with coffee and joined Linda who was already seated at the kitchen island. Linda stirred in sweetener and creamer while Carmen sipped her coffee black. Carmen sliced the bread, and Linda looked up to find her friend's concerned eyes.

"So tell me, chica, what's been getting you all worked up?" She used a fork to slice the banana bread but continued to search Linda's face.

Linda ran her fingers leisurely along the rim of the cup, then raised it to her lips to take a sip, simultaneously breathing in the aroma. She was unsure whether she should tell Carmen about the stalker. She didn't want to alarm her, but on the other hand, she thought what if Carmen was in harm's way because of someone's sinister designs against her? Her roommate should know. She should have some warning. Linda gently placed the cup back on the counter and breathed in a deep breath.

"I don't know where to begin." She shook her head, trying to hold back the tears that were forming. She had always been a strong person emotionally, but now she felt as though her strength had been knocked down a few notches. She thought that maybe she could combat the fear—if she only knew the *who* and the *why*.

"Honey, just take your time and start wherever you like." Carmen placed her hand over Linda's and squeezed it lightly.

"Someone has been stalking me," Linda confided.

Carmen gasped, spilling a few drops of coffee from the cup she held. "What do you mean?"

Linda nodded her head and began to brief Carmen on recent events, from the first day that she was aware she was being followed up to the latest phone call she had received while at the film festival.

Carmen shook her head in disbelief and lifted herself off the bar chair, hurrying out of the kitchen.

"Carmen!" Linda called after her. "Where are you going?"

She heard Carmen's voice from the other room. "We have to call the police."

Linda pushed her chair from the counter in pursuit of Carmen, attempting to try and stop her from calling the police.

Carmen was gliding her fingers over her cell phone when Linda entered the room. "Carmen, no." Linda grabbed the phone from Carmen's hand.

"No, what?" Carmen glared at Linda. "You have a crazy person running around after you, and you don't want to call the police? What's the matter with you? And what about Mr. Wonderful? He didn't encourage you to call the police on that bastard?"

"Carmen, please listen to me" Linda pleaded. "You have no idea. You don't think that I thought of calling the police? I don't have any proof that I'm being stalked. You've seen the news—the police won't do anything unless there's concrete evidence." Linda fought back tears as she continued, "I wasn't able to get a license plate number that day I was being followed, and a real phone number doesn't register on my phone when that bastard calls. So tell me, what do I tell the police?"

"Did you record the phone calls?" Carmen asked, pressing for more information.

"No, the person never stays on the phone long enough," Linda said. "It's nuisance calling. That's why I thought it was kids, but now I've been threatened."

"Threatened how?" Carmen's tone was a little more insistent.

Linda recapped the incident from the previous night out.

"So you're supposed to wait until that loony attacks you? I'm sorry Linda, but this doesn't make any sense at all to me." Carmen sat down on her bed, drawing her knees up to her chest and resting her chin on her knees.

Linda sat down next to Carmen. "I know, but unfortunately, there's nothing that I can legally do about it."

"Do you have any idea who it might be?"

Linda shrugged.

Carmen twisted her lips. "Maybe you should get a gun for protection."

"Are you serious?" Linda mouth curled into a smile. She thought back to the time when she and Carmen had gone to a shooting range to learn how to shoot a gun, and how she had the lowest score you could get. She couldn't shoot within that target to save her life. No one could understand how she had ended up with so many shots outside of it. She shook her head and looked at Carmen. "Did you forget about how on point my shooting is?"

Carmen frowned. "I fear you're hopeless in that respect."

They both laughed.

"You shoot a camera, but you can't shoot a gun. It's all point and shoot isn't it? Same thing?" Carmen asked.

Linda smiled a little as she shook her head. "Apparently not."

Carmen extended her arms. "Come here, chica." Linda gladly accepted the hug. "You'd probably shoot everybody within a fifty-yard radius except the stalker." She giggled and squeezed Linda tighter.

They held each other and laughed heartily.

Linda's laughter transformed into a stream of tears. Carmen wrapped her arms tightly around her and wiped away a few teardrops. She rocked Linda gently and whispered softly, "It's going to be okay, chica, God is not going to let anything happen to you."

* * *

Linda retrieved her coat and scarf from the closet and headed out the door. She needed to go to her studio to upload some digital images onto her computer for her latest client, Urban Styles.

The harsh wind whipped around her and blew her hood off, sending her hair about and obscuring her vision. The wind cut through her clothes like she had nothing at all on. Her body shivered from the bone chilling cold. She pulled the hood close about her face once again. New York winters could be so brutal. Seattle winters were much milder with less snow. Though she loved New York City, she didn't think that she could ever get used to this biting cold weather.

She zigzagged her way down the crowded

sidewalk, nearing the building which housed her studio.

Once inside, she pushed off her hood and rubbed her gloved but frozen hands together for warmth. She smiled and waved at Ellen, the flaming redheaded lady who sat at the information desk. The lobby was empty except for a couple who had just walked through the lobby entrance of the restaurant across from where she stood at the elevator bank.

She fumbled in her purse for the keys to the studio as she exited the elevator. She attempted to push the key into the lock, but the keychain fell out of her hand to the floor. As she bent to pick up the keys, she brushed against the door, causing it to swing open.

"Hmmm . . . that's strange," she said aloud. She made a mental note to ask the building manager if they had entered her studio for some reason.

Her hand groped blindly for the light switch on the wall. She flipped it on and gasped, "Oh my God!"

Shredded papers littered her desk and the floor. Developed prints were torn and scattered about. Protective film sleeves had been opened, the filmed pulled out of them. Desk drawers hung open.

Studio strobes and her brand new computer had been smashed on the floor.

Her heart pounded. Her body shook. She couldn't catch her breath at first, but then took a deep breath to calm herself. She pulled her phone out of her purse. Hands shaking, she dialed the police.

After hanging up with the police, she punched in Steve's number but then remembered he was at a board meeting. She decided to leave him a message anyway. She paused for a moment, closed her eyes, and took in another deep breath. Then she called Marc.

"Hey, it's me," she said as soon as he answered. "Can you come to my studio? Someone broke in here and destroyed everything."

Marc's reply came quickly. "Damn . . . Wow . . . what the hell? I'm on my way. Did you call the police?"

"Yes, they're on their way. Hurry up and get here. I'm scared." She ended the call.

* * *

Two uniformed cops arrived. One surveyed the studio while the other questioned her. Once they had enough information for their report and advised her to change her door lock, they left. She lifted the overturned chair from the floor and pulled out her phone to dial Marc again. Startled by a knock at the door, the phone slipped from her hand. As she was retrieving it from the floor, it rang. She saw from the caller ID that it was Marc.

"Where are you?" Linda could hear the panic in her own voice.

"Right outside the door. Didn't you hear me knocking?"

She swept pass the mess to the door, phone still at her ear, and swung it open.

Marc stepped through the doorway, a worried look on his face. "I'm sorry. I tried to get here as soon as I could." His eyes searched her face. Her eyes met his. Her bottom lip trembled as she tried to hold back the tears. She staggered into his opened arms, nearly knocking him over. He held her while she cried. She closed her eyes tightly, squeezing back the tears. Then he looked past her, scanning the ransacked room. "What the hell happened here?"

She followed his eyes to the piles of mess scattered around the studio. "This is what I walked in on."

"Wow. This is crazy. Who would do something like this?" He continued to survey the room.

"I don't know. It had to be the stalker."

Mark frowned and nodded.

"The police were no help. They just looked around the place, asked me did I have any clue who could've done something like this, and made out a report."

"Hmm . . . whoever it was, they sure made a mess. I hope that you had this stuff insured." He bent down and picked up a handful of shredded paper, examined it, and threw it back down.

Shoulders drooping, she slowly walked towards the middle of the room and raised her hands in the air. "I don't know what I'm going to do. Everything is ruined," she cried out. "I'm supposed to have pictures ready for that new account you helped me get. Now what am I supposed to do?" Tears escaped and trickled down her cheeks.

He closed the distance between them and pulled her close, enveloping her fully in his embrace. She buried her head in his chest and burst into uncontrollable sobs. "Don't worry. Everything's going to be alright," he said softly while caressing her back.

Releasing his snug hold on her, resting his hands on her waist, he stepped back a little and looked at her. "You okay?"

She sniffed and nodded.

He kissed her forehead softly before removing his scarf and coat and hanging them next to hers on a wooden coat rack that stood in the corner. "Let's get this place cleaned up."

"Thanks for staying to help me." She bent down and began picking up a couple of files sprawled across the floor.

Lifting a studio probe and placing it in an upright position, he said, "No need to thank me. You know I've got your back, but I can't stay too long because I have a date."

She did a double take as she stared at him, her eyes widened. "Date? I didn't know that you were seeing someone." It was more of a question then a statement.

"What do you think? I can't get a date in a city with millions of women?" He cocked an eyebrow, and his tone was a little sarcastic.

"Of course not. I just . . . I don't know. You never mentioned anyone."

Marc rose from his crouched position, shoved his hands in his pockets, and returned a hard stare.

"I'm not in a committed relationship like you and Mr. Steve, but I do get my share of female companionship."

Linda thought he sounded almost like he needed to prove something with that statement, but she couldn't figure out why. Marc's moods had always been a bit unpredictable, but by her estimation, if anyone should be on edge at the moment, it was her—not him. But to keep the peace, she didn't respond. She just returned to the task of cleaning.

They moved around the studio, picking up the litter from the floor, putting away files, tidying up her desk, and uprighting overturned furnishings. They continued cleaning up in silence. Well, not complete silence—Marc was whistling and humming, and it was really getting on her last nerve. She was already feeling a bit over the edge, and the sound only intensified her anxiety, but she figured it was better to have him there than not. She was glad that he'd offered to help out because she would've had spent too many hours doing all this alone, and she would have been scared on top of it. The more she thought about the audacity of someone breaking in, going through her things, and making a huge mess, the more the heat rose up in her neck. She cursed under her breath as she stuffed a few photos that had escaped destruction into a folder.

"Did I just hear you curse?" Marc paused and cocked his head. "I don't believe I've ever heard you use profanity."

"Never mind me. I'm just pissed off that somebody came up in here and destroyed what I've been working my butt off for." She added, "I need to get my mind off this. I'd rather talk about something more pleasant." After tucking the last file away, she faced Marc, her hands propped on her hips. He noticed her looking at him and glanced at his wristwatch, then back down to the trash bag that he had filled. "So how long have you been seeing her? What's she like?" she asked, curious.

He stopped whistling. His gaze flicked upward from the trash bag he'd just tied, and Linda could tell he was annoyed. He confirmed it with a long sigh. "What's with the twenty questions? She's just a random woman."

"Why you so touchy about it? I'm just curious. I mean, we *are* friends. Doesn't seem right that you know all my business, and I don't know any of yours."

"Well, if you must know something about her, she kind of look like you."

She was caught off guard and didn't know what to make of what he had just said. For a minute, she thought she had heard wrong. His words repeated on a loop in her head, but her thoughts were interrupted by a knock at the door.

"Are you expecting somebody?" Marc asked. He closed the distance between where he'd been standing and the door and pulled it open.

Steve brushed past him, making eye contact without uttering a word to him. Linda noticed how Marc rolled his eyes behind Steve's back. She shook her head at the exchange. She had hoped that these two, her favorite two men, would become friends. Was that asking for too much?

Steve pulled her into his arms. "I'm so sorry, baby. I didn't get your message until my plane landed." He released her and surveyed the previously ransacked room which now had some order to it, save for a few trash bags, a broken lamp, and a smashed computer screen taking up space in the corner of the room. "Did they take anything? Are you okay? What did—"

Marc interjected, "Late as usual."

Steve narrowed his eyes at Marc. "What are

you talking about? What's that supposed to mean?"

Shoulders rolled back and chest thrust out, Mark smirked, "It means exactly what I said. When you gonna learn how to take care of your woman? She got a damn stalker after her, and you're either never around when she needs you, or late coming on the scene when everything's over. If she was my woman, I—"

"Well, she's *not* your woman. You best remember that," Steve said through clenched teeth as he took a step toward Marc.

Marc snorted and moved closer, leaving less than a foot of space between the two of them.

Linda stepped in between them, flattening one palm on each of their chests. "Guys, please . . . stop it." She looked from one to the other. There was so much testosterone swimming in the air she almost could feel hair growing on her own chest.

Nostrils flared, Marc reluctantly backed away. With long deliberate strides, he crossed the room to the coat rack and snatched his coat and scarf. "Let me get the hell out of here before I hurt somebody." He swore under his breath before turning to Linda. "I gotta go. I'll talk to you later."

He stormed out of the studio, slamming the door behind him and sending the delicate wall art that hung next to the door crashing to the floor.

Linda crossed her arms over her chest and glared at Steve.

"What?" he asked.

"Why can't you two just get along?" It broke her heart that whenever she talked to each of them about the other one, they didn't seem to like each other. She was tired of playing referee between the two of them. And tonight, they had *both* gotten on her last nerve.

"Really? I can't believe you're asking me that. Did you see the way he jumped in my face?" he snapped. "I was two seconds from knocking him on his ass."

She shook her head. "Marc is like a brother to me. He's just being overprotective, that's all." She tried to be convincing to Steve, but she couldn't shake the thought of Marc telling her he was dating her twin.

Steve lifted a trash bag from the middle of the floor and carried it over to the corner, placing it with the others. "I don't like him. I never have. I don't trust him, either."

She cocked her head and raised a brow. "Do I detect a little jealousy, Mr. Mitchell?"

He closed the distance between them and took her hand in his. "Babe, I wish it were that simple. I mean . . . I would definitely be jealous of another guy spending time with you, but this guy? I question his motives for getting so close to you. You haven't even known him that long, and already he's like a brother. Just how does that happen?"

She studied him for a long moment before answering, "It happens when you don't usually connect with people. But Marc is cool people, and he's helped me tremendously with my business." Poking him softly in his chest with her index finger, she told him, "You have nothing to be jealous of, and he's not strange." She held her left hand up spreading her fingers, pointing to her ring finger like Beyoncé did in her "Put a Ring on It" video. "He just thinks that you need to put a ring on it."

Steve frowned, and his face reddened. "What business is that of his?"

As she watched his face flush with anger, she wondered what Steve was getting upset over—the fact that it was Marc who had said he needed to show his commitment to her, or that she had brought it up.

"It's not just him. My mom and Carmen feel the same way."

"I thought that this was about you and me?" He pointed his finger from her to him.

"It is." She gazed up at him intently. "But it's been two years. And I want to know where I really stand. Am I standing where I think I am?"

He stared down at her. "Marriage is a big step."

"You're making an assumption. Neither one of us have ever taken that step, so how do we know?" She picked an invisible piece of lint off his sweater.

He was quiet for a moment as he bit his lower lip. She'd noted this signature gesture whenever they'd talk about something he felt uncomfortable with. "Are you proposing?" His mouth curved into a smile.

She took the soft, squeezable stress ball from her desk and tossed it at him. "No, but when you get ready, I want a princess cut diamond, okay?"

With the backs of her thighs pressed against the solid wood desk, he moved closer and pressed his lips on hers, lacing his arms around her waist. He lowered his mouth to hers and used his tongue to part her lips. He slid his hand down her back to her bottom, filling his palm with it and kneading her firm flesh. His hardness pressing against her caused waves of heat to rise up in her. His lips clung to hers as he lifted her onto the desk, pushing a few items around to clear some room to lay her back. Her breathing became heavier, and her pulse raced. Adrenaline coursed through her body when she realized she was going to be taken right there, heightening her arousal.

Linda welcomed the lovemaking. She needed his mouth and his hands and every part of him to touch her and fill her. She needed the distraction, too, because when it was over, she'd have to come back to the reality that her stalker was no longer just making phone calls. He'd invaded her space and destroyed her work.

9

Linda was awaken by the sound of sirens blaring outside of her apartment building. It wasn't unusual to hear them in a city like New York, but the noise seemed to be coming from right outside her bedroom window. She threw her bedcovers off, swung her legs over the edge of the bed, and pushed her feet into the soft, fluffy slippers she kept next to her nightstand. She toddled across the room to the window and peered out to see what all the commotion was about. From the window, she could see an ambulance, a police car, and a fire engine, but she couldn't make out what was actually going on.

The apartment was quiet, eerily so. It was

devoid of the usual sounds of Carmen singing or playing music, and then she remembered that Carmen had borrowed the car to go to Brooklyn.

The sound of the doorbell ringing, together with frantic banging on the door, turned her attention away from the window. *What the hell!* she thought. Grabbing her robe from the hook on back of the door, she threw it on and secured the belt around her waist into a knot as she moved swiftly down the narrow hall to the door to find out who was making all that racket. She flung open the door to find a very attractive, dark-skinned man with a police shield hanging from a chain around his neck and her neighbor, Gladys, the middle-aged woman who lived down the hall. Both stood there with solemn looks on their faces.

The first to speak was Gladys. Linda was only able to make out a few words from her incoherent rambling. " . . . .it's Carmen, Linda! Oh my God!" she cried out.

Linda was temporarily stunned. "What are you talking about, Gladys?"

Linda's eyes traveled from Gladys' tear-soaked face to the impassioned face of the police officer. She read him. He had bad news. But that was to be expected because Gladys was crying. His eyes caught hers and held for a moment. Chocolate brown eyes, the color of milk duds. They seemed to do a quick sweep of her person. Subconsciously, she pulled her robe a little tighter and raised her hand to her bedhead hair.

"Ms. Bowman, may I have a minute?"

Gladys turned and walked off down the hall.

Her heart was frozen. Whatever this was . . . it was bad.

"Miss, my name is Detective Sean Gregory. Do you know a Carmen Rodriguez?"

Linda shook her head to clear the fog. Her heart was still racing, but now it wasn't because of Detective Chocolate. "Yes, Carmen is my roommate. But she's not here. What's this about?" His eyes scanned a page of the notebook that he lifted from his duty belt, then focused his attention back to Linda and asked, "Does she own a red Lexus?"

Linda felt numb as she tried to understand what was unfolding around her. Her head was spinning with questions. "Detective, would you please tell me what's going on? Why are you asking all these questions about Carmen? The car is mine.

What does my car have to do with anything? Has Carmen been in an accident?"

The detective paused for a moment, taking in a deep breath. "May I come in?"

Linda gave him a skeptical look before pulling the door open wider. He stepped into the entryway of the apartment and removed his hat from his head and held it in his hand. Linda shut the door behind him and led him into the spacious sunlit living room. She motioned with her hand for him to be seated, but she remained standing. She had a feeling he was there to deliver bad news of some sort that had to do with Carmen. Linda hoped that she was dead wrong about that. Maybe Carmen got into a fender bender, and the car was disabled. *No, that couldn't be it,* she thought. A cop doesn't come knocking on the door for a fender bender, and Gladys seemed to be beside herself in distress. What could be going on?

"Please sit," he said.

Linda wanted to say no, but a knot of fear was lodged in her throat. She shook her head.

The detective frowned his disapproval and then cleared his throat. "Ms. Rodriguez has been in an accident. She's being transported to New York-Presbyterian by ambulance."

"What happened?" Linda exclaimed.

"I don't know any other way to tell you this other than coming out and saying it."

Anxiety gripped her. She bit her bottom lip, steeling herself for the worst.

"Your vehicle exploded."

Linda's heart dropped and her stomach lurched. She tried to speak, but the words seemed sticky in her mouth. She felt dizzy. Like her feet was going to slip from under her.

"Are you okay?" the detective asked.

"Yes, I'm fine. I need to get to the hospital to see Carmen." She managed to pull herself together and led the detective to the door.

He took a business card from his wallet and handed it to her. "Please give me a call if I can be of any help."

As she wiped her body dry from the quick shower, she wished that she could wash away the guilt that had just consumed her. If she hadn't allowed Carmen to borrow her car, maybe this could've been prevented.

10

Steve

Steve used every muscle in his body to slam the racquet against the ball. He was usually up on his game of racquetball, but today Chris was kicking his butt. He couldn't concentrate on the game. Chris walked briskly towards Steve. He laid his hand on Steve's shoulder and asked, "Getting old, my friend?"

Steve picked up the blue rubber ball. "I'll show you who's getting old."

He bounced the ball on the floor once and hit it vigorously with his racquet, aiming toward the front wall. Both men ran up and down the court, swatting at the ball with their racquets until the game ended.

Chris wiped the moisture from his forehead with the back of his forearm. "I thought I had this game, but man, you came back with a vengeance."

"Not bad for an old man, huh?" Steve grinned.

"On a serious note, there's something I need to ask you. Is there anything else you want to add to the divorce papers before they're served?"

Steve took a breath and held it for a beat as he mulled over the question. He shook his head. The situation with Miriam had already been complicated enough.

He put his racquet in its case and then picked up his duffle bag and tossed it over his shoulder. He exited the court and walked down the hall until he reached his locker. Unloading his bag and racquet into the locker, he headed toward the showers. As the water spouted over Steve's body, his thoughts drifted to Miriam.

The first couple of years of their marriage was so blissful. They were inseparable and so much in love. Steve reflected upon waking up in the mornings lying next to Miriam, his front to her back, his arm looped over her waist with his face nuzzled into her long, silky red hair which smelled of jasmine. He remembered how much he loved the feeling of her naked body resting against his. He'd take his hand and caress her inner thighs moving upward slowly until he reached her core. He'd part her legs with his hand and slip his thumb in and out of her until she was moist. Then he would work his way up to her breasts, cupping them and teasing her nipples with his fingers until they were stiff and erect. She'd turn and face him, planting soft kisses around his neck while caressing him into a full erection. He liked when she would take the lead and climb on top of him, straddling him she eased herself down onto his erection. He'd pump into her as she rode him until she exploded around him.

Steve shook his head, as if by shaking his head the memories would fade and evaporate back to the place where they had come from. He adjusted the water flow from the shower head, turning his face up towards it so that the water spouted directly onto his face. He willed the water to wash away the memories, but instead another unwelcome memory channeled through his brain. Within a flash, he was flooded with the memory of the birth of their daughter, Sarah.

Sarah was beautiful, sweet, and delightful. Her

curly, strawberry blonde hair cascaded delicately around her little, round, angelic face. Her energy lit up a room.

Three years ago, a week before Sarah's fourth birthday, Steve was away on a business trip to Europe. He had planned to expedite his meetings overseas so that he would be back home in the states in time to celebrate with his two favorite girls. He was in a meeting when his cell phone vibrated against his chest from inside the pocket of his suit jacket. He ignored it the first time, figuring he would check to see who was attempting to reach him after the meeting, but it continued to vibrate, causing him some concern. He excused himself from the meeting and exited the conference room, closing the door behind him. Once outside, he removed his cell from his jacket pocket and unlocked it to see who had been calling. There had been three missed calls from Miriam. It was unlike her to call so many times, so he decided to call her back rather than listen to any of her voice messages. He drummed his fingers on his knee and stared down at the patterned carpet while he waited for Miriam to answer. When she did, anxiety permeated her voice.

"Steve, it's Sarah." Miriam was sobbing so hard her words were barely discernible.

"Sarah? What's wrong with Sarah? Why are

you crying, honey?" Steve was beginning to feel a knot forming in the depths of his stomach.

"I'm at Mount Sinai Kravis Children's Hospital . . . she has a high fever . . . and a rash across her chest . . . the doctors are trying to get her fever to break. She's had a seizure. Please come... I don't know what to do!"

"Honey, don't cry. It's going to be alright. I'll catch the next flight back to the states, okay?" Steve ran his hand through his thick blond hair, trying to keep his emotions in check as he reassured his wife. He felt helpless being thousands of miles away while his little girl was laid up in some cold hospital bed. She was fine just a few days ago. He couldn't understand what had brought this on.

"I have to go. The nurse says the doctor needs to speak with me."

There was a click, and she was gone.

He held the phone clasped between both hands, his head hanging, trying to make sense of what was happening. He felt a tap on his shoulder and looked up to see the European representative for the company, Manuel, standing over him with a look of concern.

"Is there something wrong, Mr. Mitchell?"

Frowning, Steve replied, "I have to leave right away to go home. My little girl has just been hospitalized. My wife says she's very sick."

"I see. I'm so sorry to hear about your little girl. You go to be with your family. I will take care of things here." He gently patted Steve's back

***

On the company's jet plane, en route from Europe, Steve attempted to reach Miriam several times to see if there had been any changes to Sarah's condition. He figured maybe she wasn't answering because of hospital restrictions on cell phone usage—but she'd answered earlier when he stepped out of his meeting to return her call.

Why isn't she answering? he thought. *She must know how worried I am.*

When the plane landed, Steve took a taxi straight to the hospital. He attempted to call Miriam again while sitting in the taxi—no answer. Steve bit the inside of his cheeks, something he always tended to do when he got frustrated or impatient. He glanced down at his watch, noticing the time and realizing the considerable time zone difference, and figured Miriam hadn't answered because she'd fallen asleep.

When he arrived at the hospital, he navigated his way to the pediatric unit and walked over to the nurse's station to inquire about his daughter. He must have stood in front of the lady in blue scrubs sitting at the desk for at least a good four minutes before she finally looked up from her cell phone.

"Can I help you?"

"My name is Steve Mitchell. My daughter Sarah was admitted. Can you tell me what room she's in?" As the woman punched a few keys on the computer, an older woman wearing scrubs came up and peered over her shoulders, apparently scanning the computer screen along with her. They both glanced at one another with unreadable expressions.

"Ma'am, may I see my daughter now?" Steve interrupted.

The older woman moved away from the computer screen. "Mr. Mitchell, my name is Barbara. I'm the nurse in charge. Come with me, please." She stepped away from the nurses' station and proceeded to walk down the hall.

Finally! I get to see my little girl. It's about time, Steve thought as he followed on the heels of the nurse in front of him. The nurse stopped when she came to a door a few feet ahead of Steve and entered. Steve was confused when he followed her into the room because it appeared to be a private waiting area and not his daughter's hospital room.

"Nurse, I thought you were taking me to see my daughter? I'm confused. Where's my wife?" Anxiety was beginning to stir in him.

The nurse closed the door to the room and turned to face Steve. "I'm sorry to have to tell you this, Mr. Mitchell, but your daughter . . . Sarah . . . didn't make it. The doctors did everything they could—"

"No. No. There must be some mistake! That can't be possible. Where's her doctor? You must have her confused with another patient. Where's my wife?" He felt the dread seeping into his body. He knew rationally that the nurse was being truthful, but his heart couldn't accept it. He turned his back to the nurse, tears filling his eyes.

"I'm sorry, Mr. Mitchell. Will you be okay?" the nurse spoke softly and apologetically.

Steve drew in a deep breath before turning to her. "Did my wife say where she was going?"

"After Mrs. Mitchell spoke with the social worker, her friend, the lady who was with her, said that she would be taking your wife home."

Just then, the attending doctor entered the waiting room. He had been paged. The nurse introduced the doctor to Steve and left the room, closing the door behind her. The doctor explained to Steve that the cause of Sarah's high fever and rash had been measles. When the doctor left the room, Steve sunk into one of the chairs, sobbing.

When Miriam had given birth to Sarah, they had discussed vaccinations—or rather, they'd had a debate on the subject. He had shared with Miriam information he'd researched on the topic. He had also shared things about his brother, telling her about how his parents had believed his autism was the result of the vaccination against measles, mumps, and rubella. Miriam had listened to his arguments and agreed not to vaccinate Sarah due to the possible risk of autism.

11

Marc

Marc stretched across his bed on his back, one arm behind his head, and stared up at the ceiling, thoughts of Linda flitting through his mind. He couldn't see what she saw in a man like Steve who didn't show her the attention and devotion that she needed. He reflected on the day that he and Linda had met about a year ago at an art show in Chelsea where his friend Rob's exhibits were being displayed. As Marc had strolled through the gallery, his eyes had caught an attractive, exotic woman with long, dark, curly hair that cascaded around her shoulders. The red dress she wore hugged all of her curves just right. As she stood there admiring, the pieces of art on the wall, he had quietly come up behind her, pretending he was also interested in the masterpieces hanging on the wall—but it was all a ruse. He just had a burning desire to be closer to her. She was stunning. He realized now what it meant to have your heart enflamed and your soul enchanted by beauty. He could smell her perfume, not offensively loud but just enough to awaken his senses. Every one of them.

And as he was drinking in the scent of her, she had twirled around abruptly and glared at him. "Can I help you?" she asked.

"I was just admiring the art piece." He pointed a finger towards the painting on the wall in front of them. The images just pop out." He grinned.

Linda glanced at the artwork and then back at Marc. "He's a master at making the still life subjects come to life," she said.

"Do you know Rob?" Marc asked, trying to bounce back from being caught invading her personal space.

"Yes, he's a friend of mine."

After spending the next few hours talking with Linda, Marc found himself even more attracted to her. He loved the sound of her laughter as well as the way she tossed strands of hair from her face. He'd gazed intensely at her mouth as she was talking, imagining himself devouring her luscious lips. He feared the moment when she would deliver the bad news that she was 'already involved in a relationship.' He knew that a woman of her caliber would most likely be taken and would be loyal and devoted to her man. He wouldn't have a chance in hell with her. Therefore, he had realized he had to respect that and hope that she would accept his friendship instead. His thoughts were interrupted by the sound of his phone ringing. He reached over and picked it up from the nightstand next to his bed. He didn't recognize the number in the display, but he answered anyway.

"Linda?" he repeated her name as if authenticating that it was her as he quickly rose from his bed.

"Yes, it's me. What's wrong with you? Why do you sound like that?" she questioned.

"I didn't recognize the number."

"I left my house in a hurry and forgot my phone. I'm using someone else's," she explained. "Something terrible has happened to Carmen. She's in the hospital—" she sobbed.

"Where are you? Where are you calling from?"

"I'm at the hospital. Carmen's been hurt. Can you come?"

"What hospital?"

"New York-Presbyterian."

"I'm on my way."

12

Linda thought she'd wear a path in the waiting room carpet. Carmen was in surgery, and it was taking forever. She had never felt this helpless and couldn't remember ever having experienced a crisis of this magnitude. She didn't know what to do. She found herself praying audibly, and she hoped the other people in the waiting room didn't think she was crazy.

She dug in her purse, fishing for some change to try to contact Steve one last time from the hospital's pay phone. She couldn't believe that pay phones still existed, but lucky for her they did since she didn't have her cell phone, and she couldn't keep borrowing from strangers. She had tried calling Steve several times before, and her calls had gone straight to his voicemail. He should have at least received her messages by now. She sucked her teeth and zipped her purse closed, noticing that she had no more change left.

She walked back and slumped down onto the chair where she had previously been sitting. Bored from waiting with nothing to keep her occupied, she closed her eyes and leaned her head against the wall. Soon, her head was whirling with images and conversations from earlier in the day when Detective Gregory had come to her apartment. One thing he mentioned while there stood out the most—the car had blown up. She quickly opened her eyes and immediately thought of her stalker. *No that couldn't be,* she thought. *Could the crazy person stalking her have done this?*

A few more people filled the waiting room. A big, burly man with a bushy beard sat next to her. Wrapped in his hand was a strand of rosary beads with a crucifix dangling from it. He started praying profusely for his wife. Apparently, she had been brought in from a serious car accident.

She heard his voice before she saw him. "Linda," Marc said and relief washed over her.

"Marc," she said in relief, standing and

embracing him. Holding him tight, she tried to fight back the tears that welled in her eyes. It was a losing battle.

Marc kissed the top of her head then released her just enough to view her tear-soaked face. "How's Carmen? Have you seen her yet?"

Without speaking, she shook her head in response. Tears continued falling down her cheeks. "Marc . . . this is all my fault," she said in a broken voice.

Marc tilted her face, his hand under her chin. "Why would you say that? How could this be your fault?"

Wiping tears away, along with a few tendrils of hair that had fallen into her face, she said, "Because I let her borrow my car." She lifted her eyes to meet his and continued, "I think that this was all meant for me. I should have told the police about my stalker from the beginning, and maybe this wouldn't have happened."

"Calm down and listen to me, baby girl. This is not your fault. You didn't have enough evidence to report to the police, remember? Carmen's going to be fine." He pulled her closer to him, letting her soak his shirt with her tears.

Linda felt Marc's body tense, and she

looked in the direction of his heated gaze. Steve stood a few feet away, reciprocating Marc's stare. Marc clenched his mouth, causing a muscle in his jaw to twitch as he stared back at Steve. She tore away from Marc's embrace and walked over to Steve. He snaked his arms around her.

The doctor entered the room. "Ms. McNair?"

Linda swiftly moved closer. "Yes, doctor. How is Carmen? Can I see her now?" she asked as she steeled herself for what would come next.

The doctor studied Linda for a moment. "Ms. Rodriguez's body has sustained a lot of trauma. She's been badly burned from the explosion with multiple second degree and a few third degree burns. She is sedated right now, and her condition is critical. We're in the process of having her transferred to our burn unit."

"I want to see her," Linda interrupted.

"I'm sorry, Ms. McNair, but I'm afraid I can't let anyone in to see her right now. She's in a fragile state. She's very susceptible to infection. It would be harmful to her for me to allow anyone in the room with her. Once she has been transferred to the burn unit, you can see her there." He left the room.

Linda remained standing, rooted. Motionless. Marc took a few steps toward her, but then gathered his jacket from the chair and left.

"Steve, I don't know wh— The car . . . it— How does a practically new car . . ." her words trailed off.

Steve pulled Linda back into his arms and whispered, "Shh . . . Don't worry about that right now. It's going to be alright, sweetheart, and Carmen's going to be fine."

He said the words, and she wanted to believe them, but with everything that had happened, she just wasn't sure it would ever be okay again.

13

Linda sat at the breakfast island eating an omelet and forking up cubes of melon from the bowl of fruit next to her plate. She reflected on the past two weeks. It had been two long exhausting weeks. Although Carmen had made it through multiple surgeries, the doctors said that she still had a long road to recovery. Most days when she visited Carmen at the burn center, Carmen had been sleeping and unaware of her presence. The doctors wanted to keep her pain free, and the drugs given to her for pain kept her sedated. It had been difficult seeing her usually vivacious friend in a hospital bed, immobile and breathing with the assistance of a mechanical ventilator. Her lungs had been injured from inhaling the smoke from the fire. Tears began to fill Linda's eyes as she thought about her friend's horrific incident. She was startled by the sound of her phone ringing. She picked it up from the countertop and saw the picture that she had assigned to her mother's number on the display. She pressed the button to answer.

"Hello, Mom," she answered, reaching over her plate to fork another melon cube.

"Linda?"

"Yes, Mom. It's me." She chewed quietly on the piece of melon. "Oh my God. I forgot you're supposed to be flying in tomorrow." She laid the fork down on her plate.

"That's why I'm calling, honey. I won't be coming tomorrow. I had to cancel my flight."

"Why? What happened? By the way, you don't sound too good." She wrinkled her brow.

"That's just it. I came down with the flu."

"Well, don't worry about not coming, Mom. Just take care of yourself. Feel better. How's Dad?"

"He's fine, sweetie. He's here, taking care of me," she added. "Honey? You sound like you've been crying."

Linda was silent for a moment. She contemplated whether or not she should tell her mother about Carmen. She didn't want her to go overboard with worry, especially since it was her car involved. Because of what her mother had gone through in her younger years and because Linda's real father had abandoned his family, her mother had always tried to safeguard Linda from the cruelties of the world when she was growing up. She'd had to work hard to convince both her mother and her stepfather that moving to New York was the right thing for her. She finally came to the decision that it would be better not to keep what had happened with the car from her mother because she knew she would find out sooner or later. Sylvia McNair was the type that would keep digging until she found out everything.

"Mom, something horrible has happened to Carmen. She's in the hospital."

"Oh, my goodness. What happened to her? Is she going to be alright?" she questioned with great concern.

"She's been burned pretty badly. She's had a few surgeries, and she'll be in the hospital for a while."

"What happened? How did she get burned? Was there a fire?"

Linda sighed. "The car she was in blew up." She was careful not to mention that it was her car. Her mother would freak if she knew that.

"Oh my Lord," her mother gasped.

Linda paused a moment, waiting for her mother to recover from the shock of the news. "The doctors say she has a long road to recovery. I'm just worried about her mental state. Carmen is a dancer, and her legs really took a beating in that accident. They don't know yet if she'll even be able to walk again," Linda said gravely.

"That poor woman."

Linda forked the last piece of melon as she glanced at the decorative retro clock with the quote "Dance me round the kitchen" Carmen had hung on the kitchen wall. "Mom, I have to go. I need to visit Carmen. Take care of yourself, and tell Daddy I said hello. I'll call you later."

After ending the call, she tossed the phone into her purse on the bar stool next to her. She gathered the dishes and placed them in the dishwasher, then retrieved her purse and coat. The doorbell rang. Gladys, no doubt. The woman was kind, but she was really making a pest out of herself.

Linda sighed and opened the door. She was surprised to find Detective Gregory standing there. There was something about him today that seemed different than the first time that he'd come to her apartment.

He spoke first. "I'm sorry to just show up like this, but I have some bad news."

She stepped back, pulling the door open wider as he came in. As she led him into the living room, he began to speak again.

"Ms. McNair, that explosion of your car was no accident . . . it was planted there," he said.

Linda froze in her tracks. She couldn't move. It was as if she was sinking in quicksand. She felt her body grow numb and detached like she was having an out of body experience. Although she had feared that someone had done such a horrible thing, she was now coming face to face with the reality. Her body went from numb to quivering.

Detective Gregory was talking further, but to her, it all sounded incoherent. His voice was drowned by her fear. *So it's true. My stalker tried to kill me.*

***

Linda sat in the passenger seat of Detective Gregory's car as he drove in the direction of the hospital. She listened as he explained how the police had found the explosive device attached beneath her car, manipulated so that as soon as the car engine started, it would set off a timer which then triggered the explosion. She stared out of the window, dazed, trying to take in what was being said to her.

"Linda?"

She heard Detective Gregory call her name, but it took her a few seconds to mentally come back into the car with him. She turned to him mechanically.

"I'm sorry, but I have to ask you this." He took his eyes away from the road for a second to study her. "Do you have any enemies?"

Her eyes dropped to her lap. She took a moment to respond. "As far as I know, no . . . Detective."

"Sean," he said. "I'd really prefer it if you'd call me Sean."

"Sean, I've gone over those questions in my head before and—"

He put his foot on the brake of the car, waiting for the traffic light to change from red to green, giving him a chance to glance at her. "Wait a minute. What do you mean *before*?"

Linda looked down at the purse strap she'd been fumbling with then lifted her eyes but didn't make eye contact with Sean. "I think I'm being stalked."

"What?" he asked. "Why didn't you mention it before now?" He waited for her to respond, and when she didn't, he continued questioning. "Why didn't you say something the first time I came to your apartment?"

Linda didn't know why she hadn't mentioned it at that time. Maybe because she didn't think that one thing had to do with the other. "Because I didn't think it had anything to do with Carmen's accident."

"So how long has this been going on? Have you reported it to the police?"

Linda released a long breath. "Listen, just as I've said to everyone else who's asked me why I didn't report it, I had no evidence to prove I was being stalked. So what was the point?"

"The point is that it's not a citizen's responsibility to gather evidence. That's police work. You know, we do things besides take reports and arrest people." He shook his head, and Linda sensed he was annoyed, but then she realized with his next words that it wasn't really annoyance. "A lot of women get hurt this way. Not speaking up. Trying to contain the situation themselves."

Linda heard the frustration in his voice. She felt silly now, like she should have known it wasn't right for another person to infringe on her space the way this unknown person had been doing. But it was like she'd said, she didn't have enemies, so why would she think someone would want to do her harm?

"That device planted underneath your car is an indication that someone wants to harm you—and I mean pretty permanently." He paused a moment before continuing. "When did this creep first began stalking you?" Again, he took his eyes off the road briefly to glance over at her. Their eyes met, and the car grew strangely smaller. She was attracted to him, which was strange because she hadn't been attracted to anyone since she met Steve.

They both returned their attention back to the road, Linda filling him in on the stalking events. By the time she had finished giving him the details, they had arrived at the hospital's burn center.

Linda pushed the button to release her seatbelt,

but before she could exit the car, Sean reached over and touched her hand lightly. "I'm sorry about what happened to your roommate."

She felt bad for being such a jerk to him earlier when it seemed that all he was trying to do was keep her informed on what was happening with the case of the car exploding. Maybe she had misread him, or perhaps she was just too upset the day that he came to her apartment to give her the bad news about Carmen. Maybe her thoughts had been clouded.

"Thank you. Listen, I want to apologize for the way that I've been behaving towards you. I appreciate you going out of your way to keep me informed on what's going on," she said genuinely.

With his hand still resting on Linda's, he studied her and asked, "Do you have a boyfriend?"

"What does that have to do with anything?"

"I'm sorry for the way that came out. I asked the question because it could have something to do with why you're being stalked."

Linda cut him a look. "And just what would my having a boyfriend have to do with all of this?"

"Well, since you don't seem to have any enemies, does he have anyone who has a grudge against him? Sometimes in cases like this, the perpetrator goes after a person who's close to their target person, figuring that they'll get their revenge through harming someone close to him or her. In this case, that would be you."

Linda stared out of the car window, watching people going into and coming out of the burn center building as she absorbed what Sean had just said. She had never thought of it that way before. *Who would want to harm Steve?* She thought. He was an executive at a large company. Maybe he did have people who was jealous of his position, but to the extent that they would want to harm him?

She turned to Sean and answered, "I don't think that's the case here."

"May I ask what he does for a living?" he probed.

Linda sucked her teeth. "Again, I don't see where that has anything to do with this."

"Come on, humor me. Remember, I told you I'm the cop, not you?" His tone was light, and it set her at ease a bit.

"Steve is a senior account executive of Techron Corporation. It's a software company.

"Hmmm ... He could very well have enemies. Maybe there are some people that he's crossed in business dealings or someone who's competing in business with him. Perhaps even a disgruntled employee. There are so many ways to gaining enemies in his position.

"If you're done interrogating me now, I need to go in to see my friend."

Sean smiled softly. He unleashed his seatbelt, got out of car, and walked around to the passenger door. Opening it, he extended his hand to assist her as she stepped out of the car. "Hey, I'm honestly not trying to hassle you. I just want to try and help find out who did this to your friend so that he can be put behind bars."

"I know that you're trying to do your job, Sean, but I don't have any answers."

He pulled his wallet from the back pocket of his jeans and removed a business card from it. Handing it to her, he said, "Here, take this. This is a good friend of mine. Detective Andre Moore. He's a homicide detective in the stalking unit. Give him a call and let him know about that person who's been stalking you."

She took the card that he handed to her. "But I've already told *you* everything I know."

"Yes, and I appreciate your cooperation. However, your statement needs to go on record.

My unit covers arsons and explosions." He looked her in the eyes. "He tried to kill you."

Linda shuddered at the thought of someone trying to murder her.

Sean continued, "Would you like for me to talk with him first and have him get in touch with you?"

Linda tucked the card into her purse. "Thanks for the ride. I'll call him."

She threw her purse strap over her shoulder and walked towards the entrance of the hospital, giving some serious thought to what Sean had implied. *Who would try to get back at Steve by hurting me?*

14

Steve

"Mr. Mitchell, you have a call from the hospital," his assistant's voice announced through his desk phone.

Steve had tried calling the hospital earlier to check on Miriam. She had refused to talk to him, therefore, he spoke with the staff in order to get updates on her condition. He'd only been given basic information because Miriam's therapist and psychiatrist would not go in depth due to patient-doctor confidentiality. But he needed to know that she was doing okay.

When Sarah died, Miriam had had an emotional breakdown. She had become severely depressed, and she blamed him for the death of their daughter because he had convinced her to avoid the measles, mumps, and rubella vaccination. And that was the cause of her death.

He thought back to that fateful day when he returned home from the hospital after being told that his little Sarah had died. When he entered the house, it was silent. Miriam's car was in the garage, and her friend Ann's car was parked in the driveway. He knew they were in the house, but he didn't hear a sound. He left his luggage in the foyer and searched the ground floor for Miriam. He called her name before entering each room. When there was no answer, he climbed the carpeted staircase with the ornate metal railing that led to the bedrooms. When he reached the top of the stairs, he could see light shining from Sarah's bedroom. He heard muffled sounds coming from that direction. As he entered the child's bedroom, he found Miriam scrunched at the corner of Sarah's bed, holding herself and rocking back and forth. Her eyes were red and puffy from crying. Her friend, Ann, was trying her best to console her. When Steve walked over to Miriam and attempted to reach out to her with the intention of holding her so that they could grieve together, she swatted his hand and pushed him away. "Get away from me," she screamed.

Steve took two steps back. He could see the anguish and pity in Ann's eyes. She raised a hand and shook her head in a way that sent the message—"Not now."

Not now. This was his wife. Sarah was his daughter. This was *their* loss, not hers. But then he returned his gaze to his wife. She writhed like an animal in pain. The look in her eyes was a mix of anger and anguish. Her words were barely discernable, so he retreated and let Ann handle what she assumed she could handle better than he.

Steve backed out of the room, thinking Miriam, as himself, was in shock. This was her way of handling it. Lashing out at him was natural, so he accepted it and he waited for her to move from denial, isolation, and anger to the point in the grief cycle where she'd accept their loss. But it had never happened. Miriam never got there. She spiraled deeper and deeper into an abyss of pain and anger and hatred, all directed at him.

Most days she didn't speak to him, but when she did, she let him know what she'd been thinking on the days she'd been silent.

"*You* murdered our daughter!" she lashed out at him.

She spent her days in the bedroom, clutching one of Sarah's dolls against her chest. Her tears never stopped flowing. The sobbing was endless.

One day, he had entered the room and leaned in closer to her than he'd been in weeks and begged, "Baby, please talk to me."

Miriam turned fiery eyes on him. "*You* killed our little girl! I should have never listened to your stupid advice. I hate you. Get out of here and leave me alone."

Minutes later, Ann entered the room, and Miriam had screamed again, "Ann! Get him out of here!"

Ann had claimed a seat on the bed next to Miriam, wrapping her arm around her shoulder. Looking over her shoulder, she said, "I'm sorry, Steve. Let her rest a bit." She shook her head over Miriam's shoulder, and Steve saw in her eyes what was reflected in his heart. Miriam was gone. She was not going to recover from this death on her own, but he didn't know what to do. She wouldn't talk to a therapist. She wouldn't even shower or leave the house.

One day, she had been taking an unusually

long time in the bathroom, so he decided to check on her. The door was locked, which was not so uncommon since she no longer trusted him. He tapped lightly on the door a few times and called out to her. "Miriam? Are you okay in there?" There was no answer. After waiting a few seconds more, he tapped on the door again, this time harder. Still nothing. "Miriam open the door!" he shouted. Something didn't seem right about this to him.

He shoved against the side of one of the double solid wood bathroom doors in an attempt to push the door open. It didn't budge. He kicked the door using all the strength that he could muster, and it flung open. He found Miriam on the floor, leaning against the side of the bathtub, blood dripping from both her wrists. Steve nearly toppled across the floor as he rushed over to her. He surveyed the immediate area and spotted a razor on the floor nearby with droplets of blood on it. He raced to the towel rack, grabbed a couple of face towels, and tied one around each of Miriam's wrists. Then he dashed out of the bathroom and grabbed the cordless phone, bringing it with him into the bathroom as he dialed 911. Blood was seeping through the towels he had tied around Miriam's wrists, indicating she had slashed deeply into her flesh. The color was starting to drain from her, and her skin was taking on a bluish hue. He sat on the floor next to Miriam and pulled her lifeless body to him, lifting her arms above her heart and holding them there as he talked to the 911 operator using the speaker function on the phone. He prayed that they made it there in time.

Miriam had spent over two years hospitalized, traumatized by the death of Sarah. During that time, Steve was advised not to have contact because she would become notably upset by his presence. When she was able to communicate, she made it known that she did not want to see or talk to Steve, and that she wanted a divorce. However, the doctors didn't feel she was stable enough to make that type of decision. Steve wasn't surprised by her request because, before the hospitalization, she had constantly stated that she wanted a divorce and reminded him of how much she hated him for murdering their daughter.

A sharp knock on the door jolted him from his thoughts, and his assistant opened the office door. "Mr. Mitchell, the hospital is on the line, remember?"

"Thank you."

He pushed the blinking button on his desk

phone. "Hello, this is Steve Mitchell." He paused, waiting for a response and then continued, "I'm sorry to have kept you waiting. Thank you for returning my call. I'm calling to check on how my wife Miriam is doing."

The voice on the other end responded, "I'm sorry, Mr. Mitchell, but your wife is no longer a patient here. She was discharged a couple of weeks ago."

Steve felt heat rising up in him and tried to remain calm, but he realized his attempt had failed when he heard his voice raise. "How is it that my wife was discharged from a mental institution, and I wasn't even notified?" He dropped the pen he'd been using to sign documents as he was talking on the phone. He pushed away from his desk and stood up, holding the phone to his ear as he turned to face the floor-to-ceiling windows in his office.

"Mr. Mitchell, your wife's condition had improved to where she could make her own decisions."

"So you're telling me that someone who has been institutionalized for over two years can make a decision on their own to be discharged?" he growled into the phone's receiver.

"Mrs. Mitchell no longer needed inpatient

care. Her doctor signed her release papers. So the answer to your question is yes. She's over 18 years old and no longer a threat to herself or others. It would be unlawful and unethical to hold her against her will. Is there anything else that I can help you with, sir?"

Steve clenched his jaw in fury. "Dammit," he mumbled. He pulled the phone away from his ear gripping it tightly for a moment before putting it back to his ear. "Actually, there is something else that you can help me with. Did my wife mention where she was going when she was discharged?" He knew it was a moot question as soon as the words left his lips, but he figured what the hell.

"I'm sorry, but we don't have that information."

Of course not. Steve hung up the phone without any closing courtesy. He fell back into his chair. A couple of weeks. Where the hell was she?

15

Linda donned the required gown and gloves given to her by the nurse before entering Carmen's room. She'd learned a lot about burn units in the past few weeks, and one of the lessons she'd never forget was how important it was to protect the patients from infection.

She pushed the door to Carmen's room open and was pleased to find her friend awake and sitting upright. She even appeared to have a bit of her old twinkle in her eyes.

"Hi, chica," Carmen said with a weak voice. She looked terribly fragile, but her spirit was shining as brightly as the rising sun on an early summer morning.

"Hi, you," Linda replied, relief filling her voice. "How are you feeling?" Her head was still bandaged, but some of the bruises that had covered her face were starting to fade away. Miraculously, her arms were not badly burned. Her torso had received the deepest burns.

"I've been better. The doctor tells me I was injured in a car explosion," she said, gazing blankly at Linda. Linda was unsure if she was making a statement or asking a question.

"That's right. Do you remember what happened?"

"It's a little fuzzy. Last thing I remember is walking out of the building to the parking lot."

"You were going to the parking lot to get my car—you were borrowing it—and that's when the explosion happened." Linda shifted and lowered her eyes, the guilt creeping in like a thief in the night. She now knew for sure that she was the target. Carmen just happened to be a casualty in a ploy that had been meant for her.

"But your car is new. It's not leaking oil or anything. How did it explode?" Carmen began, but then understanding seemed to wash over her. She raised a hand to her mouth. "Oh my God! Are you telling me that somebody was trying to kill me?"

Linda picked up a nearby chair and moved it closer to Carmen's bed. She sat in it, pulling Carmen's hand into hers. "No, not you . . . me." She sucked in some air, trying to gain some clarity and prevent the tears that had formed in her eyes from falling. "I feel terrible because that explosion was meant for me."

"The stalker," Carmen said. "Have they found him? What are the police saying?" She had moved a little in her excitement then closed her eyes tightly, wincing from pain.

"Let's talk about this later when you're feeling better."

"No," Carmen said strongly. "I want to know about this now. Linda, did you tell the police about your stalker? Do the police know who he is? Is that who blew up the car?" she winced in pain again.

"Not exactly." She couldn't count what she had shared with Sean because it was off the record.

"Well, what's it going to take for you? I nearly died, and you still don't think there's a problem?"

"I talked with a detective who came to the apartment the day that you were taken to the hospital. He gave me the name of a detective in the stalking unit to call." Linda straightened up in the chair, wiping away a runaway tear with her forefinger.

"Did you call him?" Using her elbows, Carmen eased up higher on her pillow.

Linda paused for a moment. "Not yet." Seeing the frown that Carmen flashed at her, she quickly added, "But I will. I promise." She wasn't ready to talk to the police just yet, but seeing Carmen's body covered with burn dressings and painted with bruises, she knew that she had to—if not for her own sake, then definitely for what that creep had done to Carmen. She owed her that much.

A nurse walked into the room, greeted Carmen, and nodded her head to Linda. She checked the intravenous bags hanging from the pole at the bedside. Then she checked the insertion site on Carmen's hand. She did a quick check of Carmen's vital signs and a sweep from head to foot. She tapped a few buttons on a handheld computer and set it down on the table at the foot of the bed. She pointed to some faces on a chart that hung on the wall in front of the bed—ranging from a smiley face to a face with tears—and asked Carmen to indicate her level of pain. Carmen pointed at a face somewhere in the middle, indicating that she wasn't in a whole lot of pain.

"Excuse me," the nurse addressed Linda. "I'm going to have to change her dressings now and get her ready for her physical therapy session."

"Oh, sure." Linda stood up and looked around the nurse at Carmen. "I'll be back to see you tomorrow. Is there anything you'd like me to bring you?" Carmen stuck her tongue out and made a face at the nurse, who was unaware of it because her back was turned. Linda chuckled.

"A bottle of scotch would be good," Carmen replied nonchalantly as she watched the nurse's jaw drop. Linda smiled, moved closer to her friend, and bent down and kissed her softly on her forehead just below the bandage. "I'll see you tomorrow."

"You will call that detective, right?" Carmen reminded.

"Yes, I said I would." Spending time with Carmen made Linda realize that this was something she could no longer put off. When Linda reached the lobby, she pulled out the business card that Sean had given her with detective Andre Moore's telephone number. She tapped the card lightly against her chin a few times, wondering what she should say. She felt awkward using the term stalking, but that was exactly what was being done to her. Fishing her phone from her purse, she tapped in the numbers from the card and waited nervously while listening to the sound of the phone ringing.

"Detective Moore," a low modulated voice on the other end said.

"Hello, my name is Linda McNair. I was given your number by Detective Sean Gregory".

"How can I help you, Ms. McNair?"

"I would like to report . . . um . . . speak with you about being stalked." She lowered her voice as a couple walked past her. She hoped that this call wasn't going to be a waste of her time.

"I see. You must have a convincing case in order for Detective Gregory to have referred you. Let me take a look at my schedule and let you know when we can meet. Would you mind holding on for a minute?"

"Sure," Linda mumbled, still not totally convinced that Detective Moore would be able to help her.

After a few seconds had passed, Detective Moore returned. "Ms. McNair, are you still there?"

"I'm here."

"It turns out that I have some free time today. In fact, I can meet with you right now." He rattled off the address to his office.

"Okay, I'll be there in about thirty minutes," she replied. She ended the call and felt surprisingly good about it. Maybe he could help her end all this drama before she or someone else got hurt.

16

It had been several weeks now since the stalker's last attempt to make contact with Linda. There hadn't been any phone calls or stalking since the car explosion. Although Detective Moore hadn't reported any progress in the case, she had begun to feel a little bit relieved that things seemed to have calmed down. Detective Moore had his team fingerprint her office and check phone records. He'd informed her that there weren't any leads, however, they would continue their investigation.

She stepped out of the elevator. Turning right, she walked down the long corridor, beautifully decorated with alabaster wall sconces. As she approached Steve's apartment door, she saw him standing in the doorway, waiting to greet her. The concierge staff member had informed him that she was on her way up. He greeted her with a warm smile as he held the door open for her entrance.

"Come on in, babe." As she crossed the threshold into the apartment, she was met by the smell of food cooking, the kind of aroma that made your taste buds salivate. Steve helped her remove the light jacket she wore. The long frigid winter had passed, and the spring weather was settling in.

"Dinner is in the oven. It'll only be a few more minutes before it's ready." He sounded proud of himself.

"Did you actually cook, or did Marla prepare it?"

Marla was Steve's full-time housekeeper, and she often prepared meals for him.

Steve held his hand to his chest as if experiencing pain. "My heart is crushed." He laughed.

Linda gazed at him for a moment, taken in by how deliciously hot he looked standing there—his shirt half opened, displaying his firm chest and muscled abs, sleeves rolled up, blond hair tousled, bright blue, penetrating eyes staring at her intensely. She loved his relaxed look. Made him seem less stressed than when he was suited up for work.

Steve waved his hand in front of her. "Hey!" he said, pulling her out of her semi-trance.

"Huh?"

"Where'd you go?" He pulled her closer to him and brushed his lips across hers as she invited his tongue between them. Their tongues did their familiar dance while his hands explored her body, moving from her lower back down to the curve of her butt.

They were interrupted by the sound of the oven timer.

While Steve returned to the kitchen to check on dinner, Linda walked into the dining room and to her surprise, the dining room table had been decorated with a white linen tablecloth, candles, and a beautiful centerpiece of miniature roses with several loose rose petals sprinkled over the top of the table.

"Can I help you with anything?" she called out to Steve as she moved closer to the table, both admiring and impressed by the romantic display.

"No, I have everything under control."

She suddenly heard the sound of music coming from the sound system in the room. Linda smiled inside because it was the Miles Davis CD that she had given Steve as a gift. She'd had Marc come with her to one of the few music stores that was still in business. Of course, since he knew it was a gift for Steve, he reluctantly came along. She could not figure out why he disliked Steve so much.

She peeked into the large contemporary kitchen. There were floating wood shelves on the wall-mounted mirror above the wet bar area, which was accented with beautiful marbled countertops. Steve was standing at the matching marbled top island, spooning food from pots and a casserole dish onto two plates.

She mosied over to where he stood. "Mmmm . . . that looks and smells delicious. What is it?"

"For you, my love, Steak au Poivre with brandy cream and asparagus," he reached over and lifted a bottle of cabernet that he had previously taken from the wet bar, "complimented by this." He grinned.

"Here, let me help you." She poured dressing onto the large bowl of salad and tossed it a few times. "Thank you for inviting me over for dinner."

He bent to kiss her forehead. "It's the least I could do for you after all that you've been through.

Besides, I owe you a good dinner anyway to make up for the dinner we missed out on several weeks ago. I wanted to make it up to you sooner, but my work schedule has been so hectic."

She helped him carry some of the food into the dining room.

She nibbled on her food as she watched Steve, who seemed to have something weighing on his thoughts. She caught him a few times staring into space.

"What were you just thinking about?" She lifted her glass of wine and took a sip from it while waiting for him to respond.

Wondering where in the hell is my insane wife, if you really must know. "Oh, nothing important. There are some structural changes going on at work, and I have to reassign some positions." He picked up his fork and knife and cut into the steak. "So tell me, has that psycho tried to contact you again? And how's Carmen doing?"

Linda waited until Steve lifted his eyes from his plate to her before answering. She raised an eyebrow. "Are you sure it's nothing that has your mind occupied? And are you trying to divert me from asking what's going on in your head by turning the tables on me?"

He lifted his napkin and wiped his mouth. "No, really . . . it's nothing. Now answer my questions," he pressed.

She propped her elbows on the table, folding her hands together under her chin. "I met with a homicide detective and made an official police report a couple of days ago."

"Homicide detective? Why a homicide detective?" Steve's voice displayed a measure of concern.

"Oh . . . I almost forgot to tell you. The detective who showed up at my door the day that the car exploded contacted me and gave me the telephone number of a detective by the name of Andre Moore. He said that it qualified as a homicide case since the stalker blew up my car—"

"Wait a minute . . . that was deliberate?" he frowned. "How come you didn't say anything? Linda, I—"

She shifted her eyes down and back up at him. She was used to Steve brushing things off as insignificant whenever she attempted to share any chaos in her life with him, so she shared with Marc instead. Besides, Steve had been busy traveling, and she didn't think he wanted or needed to be burdened with the details of what was going on. "I didn't want to worry you. You've been busy with your work, and I just didn't want to add to it."

"Someone's trying to kill you, damn it, and *that's* not important to me?" He pressed his lips tight. "I admit that when you first came to me about someone following you, I was a jerk for not taking you seriously, but since that day at the film festival, I knew it was a serious situation." He paused. "How did the police find out that the explosion was intentional?"

"Detective Gregory—that cop who came to the apartment—says that an explosive device was found underneath the car."

He sat quiet for a few moments, his face starting to flush from anger. "That's it. I'm hiring a bodyguard for you until they catch that nut job."

Linda stood up, purposely ignoring Steve's statement as she began to gather some of the dishes to take away from the table. There was no way she was going to have someone following her all over town. Steve must have lost his mind in thinking that she would. Steve covered her hand tenderly with his. "No, don't. I'll take care of these later. I just want to finish our discussion."

Linda sat back down in the chair, smoothing the table cloth with her hand and trying to find the words to convince Steve that a bodyguard was not necessary. Once he got an idea in his head, he didn't let it go easily.

"I'm going to get on the phone tonight with a resource of mine to connect me to an agency that employs bodyguards. I—"

"Steve, don't be silly. I don't need a bodyguard, nor do I want one following me around, either," she added. "Besides, as I've already told you, I'm *not* being followed anymore."

"And how do you know that for sure?"

"I don't." She brushed back a few strands of hair from her face. "But the phone calls and texts have stopped. And I don't sense that someone's following me when I'm walking down the street. You know. Things like that."

Steve studied her for a moment before he spoke. "So this Detective Moore . . . has he come up with anything?"

Linda drew in a breath. "Not yet. He says that the case is still open, and they're continuing the investigation."

"Stalkers don't just give up and move on Linda, but nice try."

She cut her eyes at Steve and was ready to retort when his cell phone vibrated. He had switched it to vibrate so that the sound of the ringtone would not disturb them. He looked down at the vibrating phone and ignored it. He wanted to continue the conversation with Linda about hiring a bodyguard to protect her while the police continue their investigation. Within seconds, his phone vibrated again.

"Maybe you should get that. It could be important."

He looked awkwardly at the display like he didn't recognize the number that appeared.

"I don't know who it is. The number doesn't look familiar. If it was business, whoever it is would have called my other number. They'll either leave a message or call again if it's important."

"Um . . . they're calling again." Linda stared down at the vibrating phone.

Steve continued to ignore the vibration of the phone, turning his attention back to Linda. Linda nudged him to answer it. "Go on. Listen, I really have to get going anyway. I don't want to get caught out in the storm. I'll see myself out."

"But I thought you were staying here with me tonight?"

"I'm sorry, baby. I have go by the studio."

She sighed. "I forgot to send an attachment along with my proposal to a potential client."

She stood up and moved closer to Steve, bending to kiss him on the lips before dashing out of the room. She was glad that the call had interrupted Steve's tirade of her getting a bodyguard. It gave her a chance to escape the conversation.

"Linda wait—" he called after her, but the sound of the door shutting let him know that she had exited the apartment.

17

Steve

He put the phone to his ear. "Hello," he said.

"So you think that I don't know about your little girlfriend?" The raucous voice on the other end of the phone was Miriam. He combed his fingers through his hair as he measured how to respond. He didn't want to risk her hanging up on him. He needed to persuade her to tell him her whereabouts, but a soft approach would leave him empty-handed.

"Miriam, where are you?" Steve used a demanding tone. He hoped his firmness would be as effective as it had been prior to Sarah's death.

He paced the floor of his living room. "We need to talk."

There was a long pause on the other end of the phone before she responded, "You put me in a mental institution after killing my little girl . . ." He looked up and blew out a silent breath. ". . . then you went on to take up with that bitch photographer. Well, your plan didn't work. I'm going to make life a living hell for both you and that bitch. Do you understand me, Steve?" she yelled into the phone. Before Steve could respond, he heard a click. She had ended the call.

"Damn it." He sank onto the sofa, fuming. Raking his fingers through his hair, he tried desperately to figure out Miriam's whereabouts. He combed his cell phone contact list until he reached Miriam's parents' number. He hadn't spoken with them since Miriam's breakdown. They wouldn't have any more to do with him because they believed he was the cause of it. He listened as the telephone rang. There was no answer. He was unsure if they weren't picking up because they recognized his number or if they just weren't available. Then, all of a sudden, a thought came to mind—or rather a person, *Ann*. If Miriam was going to reach out to anyone, she would contact

Ann. He quickly rose from the sofa, grabbed his keys from the table, and set out to Ann's house.

18

Steve

Steve merged onto FDR Drive, heading south towards Murray Hill. The rumbling sound of thunder rolling across the sky could be heard just before the sky opened up, sending a massive downpour of rain which made it difficult for him to see the road. Steve's windshield wipers were of no use in this blinding storm. He thought about pulling off the road until the rain calmed down some, but he was determined to find Miriam. He called to mind the unnerving things she had said to him over the phone. *You don't think that I know about your little girlfriend . . . I'm going to make life a living hell for both of you.* His mind did a replay of the stalking events which Linda had spoken of. Could Miriam be her stalker? He couldn't make any sense of it. He had known Miriam since high school, and he didn't believe she was capable of doing anything that would harm another person. But tonight, she hadn't seemed like the Miriam he knew. Losing Sarah had such an impact on her mental state and had changed her personality. Before she was institutionalized, she would often lash out at him, but not like today. If she had been stalking Linda, she had a motive. Steve could not figure out how Miriam had found out about his involvement with Linda—or about Linda, period, for that matter. To his knowledge, Ann didn't know about his relationship with Linda, so he ruled her out.

His thoughts were interrupted by a call coming through his car stereo system. He pressed the button on the steering wheel to answer the call. "Hello". No answer. He repeated "hello". Still no answer. "Miriam, is that you?"

"Is this Steve Mitchell?" the voice of a man on the other end asked.

"Who wants to know?" Steve hated when telemarketers called, trying to pretend like they knew him. He made a mental note to have his cell number registered on the 'do not call' list just as he'd done with his home phone.

"I'm sorry, we had a bad connection there for a moment, and you probably didn't hear me. This is detective Andre Moore."

"My apologies as well, detective, I thought that you were someone else." Steve struggled to see the road through the torrential rain. Blankets of water covered his windshield.

"I need to talk with you, but I don't want to discuss it over the phone, Mr. Mitchell. Can we . . ." And then the connection dropped.

19

The sound of the rain tapping on the window was soothing to Linda as she lay in bed, exhausted from what had been a long day. She was relieved that Carmen was going to be discharged from the burn rehabilitation center. She had previously consulted with the physical therapist in getting the apartment prepared for Carmen's transition. Smiling inside, she was also relieved she had eluded Steve's discussion about hiring a bodyguard. She had begun to wonder why she hadn't heard from him since she left his apartment, especially since he was so concerned about her safety. Feeling guilty about hurrying out of his apartment while he was on the phone, she contemplated calling him to let him know that she had arrived home safely from the studio.

She lowered the bedcovers from her shoulders and reached for her cell phone on the nightstand. She touched the speed dial button and rested her head on the pillow as she waited for Steve to answer. There was no answer. When his voicemail came on, she left a message that she had arrived home safely and would be in touch with him the next day.

Linda slid back underneath the covers and drifted off to sleep, the pitter patter of the raindrops lulling her to sleep.

She was awakened by her cell phone's loud ringtone and vibration. She stuck her arm out from beneath the covers, groping blindly on the nightstand and grabbing the phone. She put it up to her ear before she realized that she hadn't touched the button to answer. She pressed it and yawned before she answered.

"Hey, baby girl."

"Marc, hey," she replied, looking at the display to see the time. "It's one in the morning? Is everything okay?"

"I have to leave for Chicago in a couple of hours

take care of some urgent family business. We'll have to push our meeting back until I get home."

"Chicago? You never mentioned that you had family there." She rubbed her eyes and turned on the lamp.

"I thought I mentioned it to you before. Anyway, I'll fill you in when I get back."

"How long will you be gone?" She'd been so busy lately and hadn't found the time to spend with Marc except for a meeting here and there. She took comfort in the fact that he was close by if she really needed him, but with him leaving for Chicago, she had already begun to miss him.

"I'm not sure yet. It depends on how soon the situation can be resolved."

"You're being mighty cloak and dagger about it. I hope everything is okay."

"It will be."

"I'm going to miss you. Be safe."

"I will. I'll see you soon, baby girl."

The corners of her mouth lifted to a smile before she ended the call. Marc was the one friend that she could tell almost anything. In fact, she did tell him everything. She'd even discussed things with him that she had not discussed with Carmen. Marc had a way of making her feel like family.

Seconds after ending the call, her phone buzzed again. "What did you forget to tell me?" she chuckled.

"I'm still watching you," said the distorted voice and then there was a chilling laugh before the phone clicked.

Linda sprung up in bed and pulled the covers snugly around her. Shaken by fear, her heart began to race. Her chest felt as if someone had wrapped a rubber band tightly around it. Her breathing weakened. This time, she knew what kind of psycho the stalker was and what he was capable of doing.

20

After getting Carmen settled back at home from the burn center, Linda retrieved her purse and dug out her cell phone. She'd left Steve another message earlier while en route to the burn center. She checked the display on the phone to see if there were any notifications of missed calls or messages. Nothing. She furrowed her brow and attempted to call him again. It was unusual for him not to return any of her calls. Even after they'd had major disagreements, he had always responded to her phone messages. Still no answer. This time, she couldn't leave a message because his voicemail was full. She dropped the phone back down into her purse and sighed.

The sound of the tea kettle whistling reminded her that it was time to steep her tea. Carmen favored loose leaf black tea. While she waited for the tea to steep, her mind flashed back to the call she had received from the stalker. She had been so engaged in helping Carmen get transitioned that she hadn't had time to think about it. As much as she hated to agree with Steve, she now believed that he was right about the psycho not giving up. She poured the hot steamy tea into a cup and sweetened it with rose petals and walnut preserves. She frowned. The smell was strong, and not in a good way. She placed the cup on a saucer and carefully carried it into Carmen's bedroom. When she entered the room, she found Carmen sitting up in bed, watching a game show on TV. Her facial scars from the accident had healed and were barely visible. She had regained strength in her legs and arms through several weeks of grueling physical therapy. The burns on her body were gradually healing. The doctor had said that it would be difficult to tell how much of the scarring will be permanent.

"Hola, chica," she smiled at Linda. "Why the long face?"

"Must just be exhaustion. I didn't get to sleep

much last night." She tried to conceal her true sentiments. There was no way that she was going to deliver the bad news that the stalker had started harassing her again. She couldn't ruin Carmen's homecoming that way. She'd wait to tell her after she had settled in for a few days.

"Que pasa? Why couldn't you sleep?" she asked, a concerned look on her face.

Linda waved her hand, forcing a smile. "Oh, all that noise from the thunder and rain last night kept me awake."

"Are you sure?" Carmen narrowed her eyes.

"Yes, I'm sure. Now drink your tea before it gets cold." She placed the tea on a tray and carried it over to Carmen, carefully putting the tray down across Carmen's lap.

"Thanks Linda. I hope I'm not burdening you." She picked up the cup of tea and blew over it before taking a sip.

"Girl, please. Don't give it a second thought. I know you would do the same for me."

"I would?" she teased.

Linda leaned against the mahogany wood dresser with her arms folded and lifted a brow.

"Just kidding. Of course I would." Carmen

smiled brightly. Her smile suddenly disappeared. "You know, I've been thinking."

Linda moved over to the bed, smoothed the covers, and gently eased down onto the mattress, trying not to cause Carmen any discomfort. "Thinking about what?" she asked.

Carmen placed the cup of tea back down onto the saucer and pushed it to the side of the tray. "Sometimes things happen for reason. I think that God slows us down when we're too busy doing this and doing that."

"What do you mean?" She steeled herself for what Carmen was about to say.

"I had promised my family a long time ago that I was going to take some time from my dancing and go to Cuba to visit them and stay a while. I haven't seen any of them in about ten years. Dancing had become my life." Her eyes began to fill with tears. She wiped a few away and pulled some tissues from the box on the table next to the bed and blew her nose. She took a deep breath and continued in a broken voice, "You know, my father passed away, and I didn't even make it to see him before he died. I was supposed to have gotten my papers in order to go there, but I didn't get them on time because I was too busy coordinating shows for my dance troupe. Now, my mother is not doing so well. She has heart problems and diabetes—" she paused and the tears began to flow more quickly.

Linda edged closer and took a tissue and patted Carmen's face. "I'm sorry" was all she could muster. She had never seen Carmen this vulnerable before. She'd always shown so much strength and audacity, but Linda certainly understood her vulnerability due to all she'd been through in the past several weeks. A wave of guilt past through her as she watched Carmen's tearful admission of guilt for not spending time with her family when they needed her the most.

"Well, anyway, now that my dancing is over, I can make the time to be with my family. After I heal more." Carmen dried her eyes once again.

"I'm sure your family will be elated to see you. And getting away for a while may be just what you need." She smiled.

"Okay, enough about me. How are things with you and Mr. Wonderful?" she smirked playfully.

"He seems to be a little distant lately. I think he's working too hard."

"Stop making excuses for that man. If he really wanted to be with you more, he would make the time and effort." She rolled her eyes.

"He has a really demanding job. It keeps him busy . . . I knew from the beginning that our time would be—"

"And this is what you want to settle for?"

Linda had to admit that the relationship wasn't all that she had hoped for. There were still some things that she felt Steve wasn't sharing with her. Marc had implied more than once that he thought that maybe Steve was hiding something. She couldn't take everything Marc said at face value because she believed that he was speaking from an intense dislike of Steve. But although Steve had shown her kindness and care, she didn't feel the connection she thought she should be feeling. Then again, he had been more respectful and faithful than the men in her past relationships. Was she wrong for loving him more than it appeared that he loved her?

Her mother loved her stepfather more, but it had never cost them their relationship. Now that she thought of it, it had been a pattern in most of her relationships. But she couldn't help that she loved too hard and too deeply. It was the only way that she knew how to love.

21

"Yes. That's it. Beautiful. One more shot, and it's a wrap," Linda commended the young model for her effortless poses. She truly enjoyed her work as a photographer. Hearing the sound of that camera clicking was music to her ears. It was a perfect day for shooting with the sun not shining too brightly, making the lighting perfect. The day had almost been wasted when the young well-known model had shown up late for the photo shoot and further delayed everything due to her hissy fit over not getting the specific flavor of cream in her coffee that she had requested. That was the downside to having to work with models who thought the world revolved around them. Linda swiftly skimmed through the photos in her camera and was pleased with the outcome. She gave the crew a thumbs up before she packed her equipment.

With still no word from Steve, the thought occurred to her to try calling his office this time around to see if he was there. Waiting for the phone to be answered, she pulled off the elastic scrunchie that held her long, dark tresses back in a ponytail. She shook her hair out and combed her fingers through it. She couldn't ignore the unsettling feeling that something was not right about all of this.

She recognized the soft-spoken voice of Steve's assistant on the other end, "Good afternoon, Steve Mitchell's office. How can I help you?"

"Hello, Estelle, this is Linda McNair. May I speak with Steve please?"

"Oh my goodness, Ms. McNair. You don't know?"

"Know what?" Linda's stomach flipped. "He's not on a business trip?"

Lowering her voice to nearly whispering, Estelle confided, "I'm not supposed to share this, but I guess it's alright to tell you. Mr. Mitchell's been in a car accident."

Linda plopped down onto a metal folding chair

nearby and brushed her hair from her face. A lump formed in her throat. "What? When?"

"He's in the hospital. He was in a car accident the night of that bad storm." Raising her voice back to a normal volume, she said, "Listen, I have to go now."

"Wait . . . wait. What hospital?"

She made a mental note of the hospital Steve had been admitted to before ending the call. She closed her eyes briefly, taking a deep breath, and dropped the phone into her purse. Then she quickly gathered her camera and equipment together, stepped out onto the curb, and hailed a cab.

***

Linda had the taxi driver wait while she took her equipment inside her studio, then she rushed back into the cab and made the short trip to New York Presbyterian Hospital.

Questions swirled inside her head. She knew that there had to be a reason why Steve wasn't answering her calls, but never once would she have guessed that this is why. She gazed out the window, watching the passing of cars and the people walking on the sidewalks. Anxiety setting in, she began to bite her nails, something she'd done since childhood whenever she felt anxious or nervous. Her gaze was broken by the feel of her cell phone vibrating from inside her purse that laid on top of her lap. She pulled it out and read the display. It was Detective Moore. She slid her finger across the phone, sending the call to voicemail. She didn't feel like dealing with the detective and all of his questions right now. She needed to get to Steve. She needed to see if he was alright. Just the thought of him severely injured and lying in a hospital bed put her stomach in knots. She wasn't sure if she could handle it. First, Carmen, and now Steve. She prayed silently that he was okay and his injuries were not as bad as the ones she was conjuring up in her imagination.

As usual, the streets were jammed with traffic. Car horns blew, and some drivers were using their middle finger to communicate. The cab was about two blocks from the hospital, still barely moving because of the endless traffic. Linda nerves were unsettled, and she hadn't the patience to sit any longer. She paid the cabdriver and walked the rest of the way. The walk would do her good. It would calm her nerves so that she could be strong for Steve.

She hadn't expected what greeted her as the entered the room. Fresh air had not prepared her for this. She hardly recognized him. His face was swollen and badly bruised. He was unconscious. The nurse had explained that the doctors had decided it would be best to induce a coma in order to protect his brain due to the swelling caused by his head injury from the impact of the car crash.

She tried hard not to break down and cry. Just days ago, he was afraid that something would happen to her, and now here he was, so fragile, in a coma. She retrieved a chair from the corner of the room and moved it closer to his bedside. She reached for his hand, kissed the inside softly, and held it between hers. She realized that it hadn't been so long ago that she'd been right here at this same hospital holding Carmen's hand. His chest rose and fell in unison to the sound of the ventilating machine that was attached to his mouth.

A nurse came into the room and detached the nearly empty intravenous bag attached to Steve's hand, replacing it with a new one.

"How long will he be in a coma?" she asked the nurse.

"It's hard to say exactly. It all depends on how soon the swelling goes down."

"Will he have brain damage?"

"We won't know anything until the swelling has reduced." She excused herself and left the room.

Linda bit her thumbnail nervously at the thought that Steve could come out of his coma with brain damage or—even more frightening—he could remain in a coma indefinitely. No one at the hospital could tell her what had actually happened other than he was brought to the hospital by ambulance from a car accident.

Why had he gone out? she wondered. He seemed to have been in for the night when she had left his apartment. Then she remembered the phone calls. The unknown number. Someone who wouldn't stop calling.

22

Sweat dripping down her face and body, out of breath, Linda was determined to keep up the pace. Her trainer, Darren, was kicking her butt. She had to admit the time that she spent away from her self-defense classes had taken a toll on her, and she was paying dearly. She was definitely not in the same physical shape as she was before she quit. She'd made a decision to re-enroll in martial arts classes because she figured it would be better than having a bodyguard. She wondered what Steve would think of her joining the class again. She thought he would probably still prefer her to have a bodyguard. She enjoyed the workouts, though, because they kept her muscles toned and her body more flexible. Between trying to spend more time with Steve when he wasn't traveling and her own demanding work schedule, she hadn't had much time for the classes. She and Marc had taken the classes together. She believed he spent time with her in this way partly because he enjoyed watching Steve's disapproval of the two of them spending time together, but he'd become so serious about the workouts that he would reprimand her every chance he got about missing a session. Marc was so good in the classes that he had advanced to a black belt in karate and won a few trophies in tournaments.

She took a stance, waiting for Darren to throw a punch. She blocked his punch with her right arm and lifted her left leg and kicked out. Losing her balance, she fell to the floor with her leg buckled under her.

"Are you alright?" Darren hurried over to her.

"Ow. Yeah, I'll be okay. My mind just isn't here today." She wrapped her arms around her injured leg.

"Linda, you must always focus—"

"Yeah. I know. Focus, focus." She smiled through the pain she was experiencing. *I am focused. Focused on wondering what the hell is happening in my world.*

Darren had her release her leg from its bent position, and he massaged the area where she felt the pain. It had begun to feel better almost immediately. If only she could bottle those healing hands.

He helped her stand, and she took the stance position again when the pain returned rapidly as lightening, causing her leg to almost buckle.

"Okay, that's it for today."

"I'm fine. I can push through the pain. Let's finish." She shifted her weight on the unaffected leg.

Darren looked at her like he wasn't buying it one bit. "Are you nuts? I'm not going to be responsible for you injuring yourself worse than what you already have."

"C'mon Darren," she petitioned. "I can handle it. I can tough it out. It's not that bad." She placed her hands on her hips, trying unsuccessfully not to wince from the pain. She couldn't understand what was driving her to keep going, but whatever it was, she needed to continue even through the pain. She needed to do something to free her mind of the chaos that seemed to be taking over her life.

She felt so out of control of the things happening around her. At least if she could control the pain, then she'd controlled something.

"Seriously? Not on my watch. Take care of that leg and let's see how you feel in a few days." He walked away and left her standing there.

Linda waltzed past him, rolling her eyes at him and stumbling a little but swiftly regaining her balance. She glanced over her shoulder to see if he had witnessed it. *Just wait until I get myself together, Darren. I'm going to come back here and wipe that damn smirk right off your face.* She smiled inside at the thought of it.

When she reached her locker, she opened it and pulled out her gym bag. She reached inside to retrieve her cell phone. She wanted to check to see if there had been any messages from the hospital. She had asked the nurses to let her know if and when Steve's condition has changed. The phone screen informed her that she had several messages. She put in her code and listened to each one. No messages from the hospital, but Detective Moore had left one. Something about he'd been trying to contact Steve. What for, she wasn't for sure. Must be part of his investigation to interview everyone close to her. After listening to all of her voice messages, she reviewed her text messages. She had received a text message with a picture of her bedroom, and the caption read SWEET DREAMS. She didn't recognize the number that it had been texted from. The hairs raised on the back of her neck. *It must've come from that bastard who's stalking me.* Her hand trembling, she dropped the phone.

"Linda? Are you okay?" she heard a familiar voice calling to her. Her eyes opened slowly to see Darren looking down at her. She could hear soft murmurs in the background. Her eyes looked past Darren, surveying the room. There were a hand full of gawking onlookers. Slowly gaining consciousness, she began to blush from embarrassment when she realized she was lying on the floor, apparently from falling.

Her head felt like someone had taken a baseball bat to it. She lifted her arm and touched the part of her head where she felt the pain most intensely. When she withdrew her hand, she saw blood. She must have hit the floor pretty hard.

"Linda?"

She focused her eyes on Darren. "Yes," she answered in low voice, almost a whisper.

"I've called an ambulance. They're on their way."

Still kneeling at her side, he reached for the towels being handed to him by one of the onlookers. He rolled them together and tucked them gently underneath her head. "Here, rest your head on this until the ambulance gets here."

"No ambulance," she moaned.

"You've been hurt. Your head is bleeding. You need to be looked at," he said.

The ambulance had arrived, and one of the emergency medical technicians approached them and kneeled down, replacing Darren's position.

"Hi there. Can you tell us your name?" He removed a pouch from the bag that he sat on the floor next to him. "I'm going to wrap this around your arm to take your blood pressure."

Meanwhile, Darren cleared crowd from the area.

"My name is Linda. Linda McNair."

"Can you tell me what happened, Ms. McNair?"

"I'm fine. I just fell and got a little bump on my head. That's all." She winced attempting to sit up from the floor, and quickly realized she'd be better off resting there just a bit longer until the pain subsided a little more.

"Did you lose consciousness when you fell?" he swiftly surveyed her from head to toe, searching for any visible injury, swelling, or bruises, at the same time monitoring her mental state.

"Yes, she did," Darren affirmed. "I don't know how long she was unconscious, but I can tell you that she left the exercise room about five minutes before someone alerted me that she was lying on the floor, unresponsive. Prior to that, she had pain in her left leg during our workout, but nothing that would have caused her to faint."

The technician took into consideration what Darren had told him before turning his attention back to Linda. "What were you doing just before you passed out?"

Linda gave the question some thought. "I was looking through my—oh my God! I have to get to Carmen." She pushed herself up from the floor.

"Take it easy. Who's Carmen?" The technician held his hand to her, trying to prevent her from standing.

"She's my roommate. Let go of me. I have to go!" she yelled, attempting to get free from his hold.

"You're not in any shape to leave here alone."

"You don't understand—she may be in danger."

"Why would your roommate be in danger?" he looked at the other technician, who shrugged.

"Ma'am, since you've experienced a loss of

consciousness, we're going to have to take you to the hospital so that you can be evaluated. You should get an x-ray to make sure that everything is okay."

"There's nothing wrong with me. Nothing more than a bump on my head." She finally got loose and stood up. Upon standing, she felt a little lightheaded. She slowly walked over to the bench and sat down, leaning her head back against the wall.

"Ms. McNair, I think it would benefit you if you let us take you."

"I'm not going to the hospital. I just need a few minutes to get myself together." She sucked in a couple deep breaths as if they gave her strength.

"Are you refusing to go to the hospital?" The technician had now become impatient.

"How many times am I going to have to tell you? I . . . am . . . not . . . going . . . to . . . the . . . hospital," she grimaced.

"Linda, are you sure that you want to do that? Why don't you just go with them and get an x-ray just to be sure?" Darren seemed concerned.

"Really, I'm okay. No need to worry, Darren." Linda turned to him. "Where's my cell phone? I remember dropping it." He handed her the cell phone given to him by one of the people who'd found her unconscious on the floor.

She touched the speed dial number for Carmen. Drumming her fingers on the bench, she waited for the phone to ring. *Come on, Carmen, answer.* No answer. The call went straight to voicemail. She left a message. Worried that something terrible had happened, she searched her phone for Detective Andre Moore's number.

23

Steve

Steve's eyelids fluttered open. His eyes searched the unfamiliar, cold room. He heard voices from outside the room but couldn't hear what they were saying. The smell of antiseptic hung in the air. He tried to focus his eyes so he could see more clearly. He turned his head slightly and noticed side rails on his bed. He attempted to move his arms but he couldn't. They felt like dead weight. Legs. Nope. They wouldn't move either. *Am I paralyzed?* He lay still. It felt like the room was starting to spin. His eyesight had become blurry again, and objects in the room were taking on fuzzy shapes. A figure appeared, peering over at him. It seemed to be the form of a woman, but he couldn't tell if she was real or just a figment of his imagination. The woman came closer. His sense of smell increasingly awakened as his nostrils filled with a familiar rich, deep, floral fragrance.

Miriam?

He tried to speak out, but the words would not escape his mouth. He felt like a prisoner locked inside his own body. His eyes met with an object descending upon him. When it reached him, he could feel the softness of it, but it began to press firmly into his face, preventing him from breathing. His heart raced as he desperately struggled to breathe.

24

Dashing out of the cab, she rushed to the building and unlocked the steel door in record time. Detectives Andre Moore and Sean Gregory raced after her. She could hear them calling, but she couldn't afford to waste any time. She had to get upstairs and see if Carmen was okay. Rather than wait for the elevator, she ran up the five flights of stairs, both detectives trailing her.

When they exited the stairwell and reached her apartment door, Detective Moore tugged at her arm, asking her to stand back and let him and Sean enter the apartment first. She waited while they went in. She heard Carmen scream out, "Who the hell are you? Get out of here before I call the police."

Linda rushed into the apartment. They were showing Carmen their police shields and trying to calm her.

She was holding her chest, her eyes widened, when Linda entered the room.

"Carmen, are you alright?" She hurried over to her friend and put her arm around her shoulder.

Detective Moore and Sean searched the apartment for any evidence that could have been left behind by the stalker while Linda stayed with Carmen, who seem to be still confused about what was going on.

"Linda, why are these cops here? I don't understand?" Her voice was shaky.

"How come you're not answering your phone?"

"You answer my question first," she demanded. Her eyes were filled with fear.

"Come, sit down." She motioned towards the soft cushioned sofa in the living room.

"I don't want to sit down. I want you to tell me what the hell is going on," she growled. "The cops burst in here from out of nowhere, scaring the shit out me, and you expect me to be calm?"

"I don't know how to explain this to you. I didn't want to—"

"That's your problem, Linda. You keep things from me until it's too late. Look at what happened before. Look at me!" she yelled, pointing to the burns on her body. Her body trembled, and the tears that had formed in her eyes slid down her face as she sobbed out loud. It seemed as if all the emotions she'd kept bottled up were finally being released. It pained Linda so much to see the hurt and anguish she'd caused Carmen.

When she felt it was okay to touch her, she carefully pulled her into a tight embrace and sobbed along with her. "I'm so sorry, Carmen." She guided her over to the sofa where they both sat down. They sat still and embraced without words, unaware that the detectives had finished their search and were standing a few feet away.

Sean cleared his throat. "There doesn't appear to be anything left behind. We also checked the entrance door, and there was no sign of forced entry."

Carmen looked at Linda, her eyes questioning.

Linda nodded at Sean then turned to Carmen. "The reason I asked you about your phone is because I tried to reach you several times today."

She lowered her eyes to her lap, picking at invisible lint. "I got a text message from someone I believe was the stalker. It had a picture of my bedroom."

"Oh my God. He was here?" Carmen gasped.

Linda continued, "I don't know. I was scared because I thought he might've been here and that you were in danger."

Detective Moore sauntered over and took a seat in a nearby chair. "May I call you Carmen?"

Carmen nodded her head.

"Carmen, were you in the apartment all day?"

"Yes. Wait . . . I went downstairs to pick up the mail from the mailbox and when I came back up, I saw Gladys in the hallway. She invited me in for some coffee."

"How long would you say you were out of the apartment?"

She gave the question some thought before answering, "Probably for about two or three hours because Gladys can talk your ears off."

Sean agreed, "She sure can."

Detective Moore glanced curiously at Sean.

"I had the pleasure of meeting her when I was here several weeks ago," Sean added.

Detective Moore turned his attention to Linda. "Although we didn't find anything unusual in your bedroom, would you mind checking to see if there's anything out of place from when you were last in there?"

Linda lifted herself from the sofa and strolled down the hallway to her room. Sean followed her inside.

"Was today the first time that this stalker made contact with you since the car explosion?"

Without answering him, Linda surveyed her bedroom, looking for anything that appeared to be out of place.

"Linda?"

"What?"

"You haven't answered my question. Is this the first time?"

"No, alright?" She slammed a dresser drawer shut, turning to face him.

He leaned against the frame of the door, tightened his jaw, and looked hard at her with those dark penetrating eyes. She'd seen him tighten his jaw before when he got frustrated with her that day in the car.

"Need I tell you how serious this is? I thought that we were clear on this?"

"I just want it all to go away." She dropped her body down onto her bed.

"So let me get this straight. Your life is in danger, and you think that by withholding information from the police, it's going to make it all go away?"

"Of course, I don't. It's just that I—"

"Make no mistake, this jerk is dangerous. You're not only putting yourself in danger by not revealing every time this psycho contacts you, but you're involving others like your roommate. You see how shaken she was at the mere thought of someone breaking into this place. It's selfish of you not to think of her, too."

Linda's look hurled daggers at him, but she had to admit that he was right. She felt so split down the middle on this. A part of her was terrified of the stalker, but the other part of her was naïve and foolish—maybe hopeful—thinking the stalker would get tired of calling her and move on to someone else. It would all disappear, just like waking up from a nightmare. She had tried to spare Carmen any worry by not divulging the fact she'd received another phone call weeks after the explosion, but apparently, she seemed to have made things worse. She'd meant to return Detective Moore's phone call on several occasions to tell him about the call that she'd received. But when she heard about Steve's car accident, she

183

became totally focused on making sure he was being cared for properly. Consequently, she'd just pushed it to the back of her mind. Truth be told, there was no need for her to be upset with Sean for forcing her to face reality.

"I know. You're right," she muttered. "It was a couple of weeks ago. I had just hung up with a friend of mine, Marc. As soon as I ended the call with him, my phone rang again. I thought it was him calling me back, but it turned out to be the stalker on the other end of the line."

"Hey, look at me." He moved from the doorway, closer to Linda but still maintaining some distance. "I know that you're going through a tough time with all of this, but you have to let us know any time this guy tries to contact you. If you don't feel comfortable calling Andre, then call me. But you can't keep this kind of information to yourself. It's way too dangerous."

When they returned to the living room, Carmen was smiling at something that Detective Moore had said to her. *Detective Moore must be some kind of charmer to get Carmen smiling like that,* Linda thought.

"Would you fellows like something to eat?" Carmen asked, standing up from the sofa and smoothing a few stray hairs that stuck up from her sleek, shiny hair.

Detective Moore also stood, combing through his thick hair with his fingers. "That's very nice of you, but we really must get going," he said, signaling Sean with a glance.

"New York's finest," the words escaped from Carmen's mouth, seeming a little bit embarrassed after the fact.

"By the way, what are you two doing together? I didn't know that you worked with each other directly," Linda asked, curiosity getting the best of her.

"Actually, we weren't working, Andre and I were meeting on a personal matter when you called him." Sean scratched his chin and exchanged a glance with Detective Moore.

Detective Moore turned to Linda. "Oh ... I almost forgot. I tried reaching Mr. Mitchell a couple of weeks back because I have a few questions I need to ask him. We were on the phone, and we got cut off. I've tried to reach him several times since, but he hasn't returned any of my calls. Do you know how I can get in touch with him?"

"He's in the hospital," Carmen blurted.

Both Detective Moore and Sean eyes diverted from Carmen to Linda, waiting for a response from her.

"The night of that big storm, Steve was out driving and —"

"Yes, that's the night we were on the phone. I figured the call got dropped due to a bad connection because of the storm. I'm sorry. Go on."

"His car was hit head on by another car, and now he's in the hospital in a coma," Linda said sadly.

"Wow, I'm sorry. Did the hospital say how long he'd be in a coma?"

"The doctors aren't really sure. They say it could be days, weeks, or even longer. They have no way of pinpointing it. Why do you need to talk with Steve?"

"In short, when I handle cases such as yours, I like to investigate all parties connected to the victims."

"How come you haven't investigated Carmen or Marc?" Curiosity had set in.

"I've already spoken with Carmen." He offered Carmen a small smile, and she grinned back at him widely. "I've left messages at the number that you listed for your friend Marc, but he hasn't returned my calls. Why is it that nobody wants to call me back? I'm starting to get a complex." He chuckled.

They all laughed.

Closing the door behind the two men, Linda followed Carmen into the kitchen and sat down at the island with her arms folded. "How are you holding up?"

Carmen removed two wine glasses from the cupboard, placed them on the island countertop, and poured some wine in each. She handed one glass to Linda and lifted the other to her lips, taking a sip. "I'm fine, chica. How are you holding up?"

Circling the rim of her wine glass with her finger, Linda admitted, "I've seen better days."

Linda caught Carmen staring at her forehead. "What the hell happened to you?" Her eyes then travelled down to Linda's clothes. "And why are you wearing dirty clothes? You look like a mess!"

"Not you, too," Linda frowned. "I fell in the gym and bumped my head. But I'm fine now."

"Oh, I almost forgot to tell you. Marc came by earlier looking for you. He says that he'll call you later."

"I thought he was still out of town. Why didn't

you say he was here when Detective Moore and Sean were here?"

"Sean? You're on a first name basis with that handsome hunk?" she teased.

"The day that he drove me to see you, he insisted I call him by his first name."

"Hmmm . . . I saw the way he kept looking at you," she sung the words. "I think that fine brother has the hots for you."

"No, he doesn't. Besides, he knows Steve is my boyfriend. Seriously, Carmen, I can't believe you're talking this way while Steve is laid up in the hospital in a coma."

"With all due respect, I'm not a fan of Mr. Wonderful. Nonetheless, I honestly do feel bad about what's happened to him. I'm not going to sit here and be phony because I hate it when people are phony about how they feel about someone when something happens to them. I just never liked the way that he treated you. You deserve better." She took another sip of wine.

"Steve loves me, and he treats me wonderfully. He cares about me and respects me. He even prepares romantic dinners. Before his accident, he had even planned to hire a bodyguard to protect me from the stalker. He—"

Carmen reached over, took Linda's hand, and pointed to her ring finger. "Okay, then where is the ring that belongs right here on this finger? Huh?"

Linda pulled her hand away from Carmen and shook her head. "You're impossible."

"Is that your cell phone I hear ringing?"

Linda raced out of the kitchen to retrieve her phone. She didn't want to miss any calls from the hospital updating her on Steve's condition. She picked the phone up from the oak table in the foyer and saw it was the hospital. *Finally, some good news for a change.*

25

Linda strolled over to the nurse's station. "Excuse me? My name is Linda McNair, and I got a call earlier to come to the hospital. The person on the phone didn't go into detail. She just asked that I come to the hospital. I had previously left a message to be called if Steve Mitchell's condition changed," she explained, pointing to the room across from the nurses' station that Steve had previously occupied. "I was just in his room, but he's not there. Did he come out of the coma? Was he moved to another room?"

Looking over her spectacles, the nurse at the desk asked, "Are you a family member?"

Linda scrunched her eyebrows together and

tipped her head to the side. "No. I'm his girlfriend. I've been up here visiting him daily. I was the one who asked to be called when his condition changed, and about an hour ago, I got a call telling me to come here."

The nurse glanced over at the doctor who had been standing nearby making notes in a chart. He lifted his head briefly and returned to writing.

Linda's heart began beating at an accelerated speed. Something wasn't right.

"What did you say your name was again?"

"Linda McNair"

"Ms. McNair, I don't know any other way to tell you this other than just coming out and saying it. First of all, I apologize for the person who called you to come to the hospital. Whoever it was should've checked first to see if you were the next of kin—"

"Next of kin? What are you talking about?" Linda's voice quavered. *Oh God, please don't tell me. They only use 'next of kin' when—*

"Mr. Mitchell died earlier today. I'm sorry to have to —"

"No! Please tell me that's not true! It can't be true!" she shouted hysterically. "My Steve isn't gone. He was moved to another room. He must have come out of the coma. Where is he?"

"Ms. McNair, I'm very sorry for your loss, but please calm down. This is a hospital. You'll upset the other patients."

Sobbing out loud, Linda walked down the hall of the hospital, entering each room she passed in search of Steve.

The nurse called after her, "Ms. McNair you can't go into other patient's room. Come back here." The nurse looked over her shoulders and asked the other woman sitting at the desk to call security, then she left the nurses' station in pursuit of Linda.

* * *

While Linda was being held in the security office of the hospital, the social worker who had contacted her by phone appeared. She talked with the manager of the hospital's security and convinced them to release Linda due to the nature of the situation, then guided Linda into a private room where they could sit and talk.

She motioned for Linda to sit down in one of the cushioned chairs as she sat down across from her. "Ms. McNair, I apologize for what you've been through. I had the intention to meet you when you arrived, however, I was called away to another urgent matter. Are you alright?"

"I still can't believe that Steve's gone. What happened?" Linda asked, searching the woman's face for answers.

"I'm really sorry, but I'm not at liberty to divulge any information because you're not a family member."

"Well, I'm probably the one who will be making arrangements for him. I don't understand why you're all treating me like I'm a stranger. I've been here every day since he was admitted and—"

"Honey, I'm afraid the hospital won't be releasing his body to you. His body is in the process of being released to a family member," she said.

"What? Who?" she asked, bewildered. "I don't understand."

"I wish I could give you all the details. All I can do is give that family member your phone number and ask her to call you."

"*Her?* Who was she? Steve had never mentioned having a sister or brother. His mother was deceased, and he was estranged from his father."

"Again, I'm sorry, Ms. McNair. I wish there was more I could do. If you need grief counseling, I can refer you to one of my colleagues and—"

"I don't need counseling, I need answers. None of this makes any sense to me." She sprung to her feet, chest heaving, anger momentarily replacing sorrow.

A blend of emotions crept up inside her, taking over her thoughts and sending her mind into a whirlwind. She stormed out of the hospital and hailed a cab. She didn't know where she was going or what to do with all the emotions spinning around inside of her head. Who was this family member the social worker had talked about? Why hadn't Steve told her about this woman?

"Where to, miss?" asked the cab driver.

"I don't know. Just drive." Her voice was wobbly.

The cab driver shrugged and drove off.

She let her head drop against the backseat. She felt the hot tears stinging her eyes. She knew it wasn't going to be easy, but giving up wasn't an option that she was willing to accept.

26

The alarm clock buzzed loudly. Linda reached over to hit the snooze button, knocking the clock off the table. She felt like she'd been put through the ringer. Her head was throbbing, and she had a sick feeling inside her stomach, the kind that you get after eating a full meal then taking a ride on a roller coaster. The impending eruption inside her was coming full speed. She hurried into the bathroom after climbing out of bed, stumbling and falling to the floor on the way. She struggled to get up. Too late. The contents of her stomach gushed out onto the floor, immediately infiltrating the room with its noxious odor. There was a light knock at her bedroom door. Go *away!*

"Linda, are you okay in there?" Before she could answer, Carmen had already opened the door and walked over to her aid. She tried the best she could to stoop down but was having difficulty. She wasn't yet functioning at one hundred percent.

"Carmen, no. Don't bend down here. I'll be okay," she muttered, her jaw pressed against the hardwood floor.

"I'm going to get that bloody mary I made for you. I figured you'd need it when you woke up this morning." She shook her head and left the room.

Linda managed to lift her body from the floor to a sitting position, wiping the side of her face with the backs of her hands. She heard the doorbell ring. She could hear Carmen greeting Marc.

Carmen returned to the room with Marc trailing behind her. He peeked around Carmen. "Hey, baby girl."

Raising herself up from the floor, Linda asked him, "What are you doing here?" She held her hand to her head, winching. The throbbing in her head seemed to have increased. She moved slowly towards the bed, still holding her head, and sat on the edge of it.

"You don't remember?" he laughed softly.

"Marc, I have no idea what you're talking about, and my head aches too much to try and figure it out."

"Last night. You called me to meet you. You had taken a cab to that bar Angel's Share in the East Village, and by time I got there, you'd already had a few drinks. You conned me into letting you have one more before we left. " He sat down next to where she had just seated herself on the bed.

Carmen returned with a bloody mary in her hand. She sat the glass on the table next to the bed and stood in front of Linda. "I think you should go and take a shower then drink this. You'll feel so much better."

"You two are making me dizzy in here. Marc, I don't remember calling you last night," she mused. "In fact, I don't remember too much at all about last night. I don't even know how I got home or in bed for that matter."

"I brought you home, and I helped Carmen put you to bed. You were so messed up."

"Go, chica. Go get in the shower. You smell

really bad—I can't take it much longer. You can talk when you finish." She nudged Linda to get up.

Linda slid off the bed and strolled out of the room.

The water felt so good sprinkling down on her body, soothing her skin with each drop. With her back to the spray, she leaned her head back into it, letting the water run down her head and soak her hair. She reached for the bottle of shampoo and poured a small amount into the palm of her hand, massaging it into her hair. Suddenly, her thoughts were flooded with the events of what had happened the day before, including the news of Steve's death. Tears mingled with the water that streamed down her face. Darkness had crept up inside her again. The weight of the pain lay heavy on her chest, like a block of cement making it difficult for her to breathe in the air she needed. She remembered the pain and the anger she was feeling when she left the hospital. It was as if her world had crashed down around her. Her existence as Steve's girlfriend no longer had value. It hadn't mattered that she was the one at the hospital each and every day helping the nurses care for him. Where had this family member been as she sat holding Steve's fragile hand each day, praying to

God that he would come out of the coma and live a normal life? She remembered that she had wanted so badly to numb the pain. She wasn't much of a drinker, but she'd needed something—anything—to take away the pain. Instead of going home, she'd had the cab driver drop her off at Angel's Share where she and Marc met once in a while for happy hour.

She turned the water off and grabbed a towel to dry herself, pulling another one off the shelf to wrap her hair. She didn't know how she was going to make it through the day.

By the time she had returned to her bedroom, it had been cleaned up and smelled lemony. Initially, the smell made her a wee bit nauseous. Carmen pointed to the drink she had sat on the table. Placed next to the red concoction was a bottle of aspirin. She gave Carmen a sideways look before she walked over and lifted the top from the pill bottle, plunked two aspirins in her mouth, and then took a few sips of the bloody mary. She scowled at the spicy peppery taste. Getting drunk wasn't a habit of hers, and she definitely didn't think she'd ever develop a taste for this drink.

"Linda, I'm sorry to hear about Steve. It's

no secret that I disliked the man, but I wouldn't wish death on anybody."

Linda nodded in appreciation of Carmen's comment.

"Did they tell you what happened? I mean, how did he die?" Marc inquired.

"No. They wouldn't tell me anything because I'm not his next of kin. I can't even make arrangements for his burial because I'm not allowed access to his body," she said as tears formed. Her voice was thick with emotion.

Carmen rubbed her back gently. "Does this mean that he's . . . I mean his body's still at the hospital waiting to be claimed?"

"No. That's the thing that gets me. The social worker who spoke with me and said that a family member claimed his body. His mother died, and he doesn't speak with his father. So I have no idea who this person could be."

"Don't worry. We'll figure it out, chica." Carmen cupped Linda's chin.

The sound of Marc's cell phone chiming startled her, and she almost spilled the drink. After he answered the call, Marc's voice went low, almost to a whisper. Linda exchanged glances with

Carmen, who shrugged. Marc ended the call and announced he had to leave.

"I'll check on you later, baby girl." He deposited a soft kiss on Linda's forehead and turned to Carmen, saying, "Later, Carmen," before swiftly exiting the room.

"What was that all about?" Linda asked Carmen.

"The heck if I know. That's your strange-acting friend."

Linda's cell phone vibrated against the table. Carmen reached over, picked it up, pressed the answer button, and handed it to Linda.

"Hello," Linda answered.

"You're next" was the response from a female voice on the other side of the phone.

The color from Linda's face drained rapidly. She was still holding the phone to her ear when Carmen grabbed the phone and yelled into it. "Hello, who is this? Hello?"

"Linda, your face is so pale. Who was that? Was that the stalker?"

Linda's eyes slowly met Carmen's. "My stalker is a woman."

27

In a blue funk, not caring whether she lived or died, Having no desire or strength to do anything, Linda laid in her bed for days. Her heart was torn into pieces, and she wondered if it would ever be whole again. Nightmares invaded her sleep which caused her to awaken screaming while she shivered in a cold sweat. She would not get out of bed to bathe or brush her teeth. The only reason she ate was because Carmen would bring food in to her and force her to eat by threatening to allow visitors in to see her if she didn't. So she nibbled a few bites, just to get Carmen off her back. Carmen tried to get her to go and talk to someone professionally for grief counseling, but she refused. She had turned off her cell phone and had stopped taking calls from everyone. She even refused to see Marc when he came by a couple of times to see how she was doing. She just wanted to be left alone.

Before imprisoning herself in her room, there had been a few times where she'd called Steve's workplace to try and get information about his funeral services, but her calls went unanswered. She went so far as to show up at his office twice, but she was asked to leave. She couldn't understand why she was being treated this way. She hadn't been a stranger to Steve's workplace nor to his assistant, but for some reason everyone was now treating her as if she had been responsible for his death, and she couldn't figure out why. She had gone back to the hospital to ask that social worker to have the mysterious family member contact her, but she never received a phone call.

A piece of her soul was lost. She felt caged in darkness, cold and empty inside. There had been no closure with Steve's passing. She hadn't even been granted the opportunity to say good-bye to him. She missed him terribly. There were a few times when she listened to telephone messages that he had previously left her just so she could hear his voice again. She spent long hours staring at the framed pictures of him that sat on her dresser. She'd cried out to God in anger and submission. Her eyes were dry—she'd shed so many tears that there were no more left to cry.

Her thoughts turned to her stalker. *A woman.* It had been hard enough trying to figure out why she had been targeted by a stalker in the first place, but a woman? Even Detective Moore was a little surprised to find out that the stalker was actually a woman. He said it's not unusual, but in her case, it was unexpected.

Detective Moore asked what the woman had said, but Linda couldn't remember her exact words. She had only been able to tell him that it was a woman's voice. She replayed that disembodied voice in her head over and over again to see if she somehow recognized it. *Never heard it before.* That's it! The words that the woman had said were 'You're next.'

She pulled the bedcovers back and rolled out of bed. *Now if only I could remember where I put my phone.* Her eyes surveyed the room, and she spotted it underneath the cushioned bed bench where it must had fallen off as she tossed and turned in the bed. She lowered herself to floor, extended her arm to reach it, pulled it from underneath the chair, and turned it back on to make a call to Detective Moore to see if there was any new information.

She dialed his number and waited for him to answer.

"Detective Moore."

"Hi, detective. This is Linda."

"Ms. McNair. You have impeccable timing."

"Really? Why is that?" Her curiosity piqued.

"I have something to discuss with you, but I think it would be best if we talked in person."

"Did you find out more information about my stalker?"

"I'll fill you in when I see you. Would you like for me to come there, or is there some place where you would like to meet up?"

"I need to get out of this apartment and breathe in some fresh air. How about if we meet at the coffee shop on the corner of Broadway?" She'd already begun rummaging through her closet in search of what she'd wear. She pulled out a pair of blue jeans and a long sleeve T-shirt. She grabbed a complementing flowered print silk scarf to accessorize. Even in her gloominess, she wanted to appear decent.

After a quick shower and a little application of makeup, she dashed out the door.

* * *

Andre was already seated when she arrived. She walked over, hot tea in hand. His wide smile displayed his pearly whites. He had grown a little stubble on his face which made him look even sexier. As she neared him, she could smell the woodsy scent of his cologne. Not overbearing, just enough to tantalize your olfactory senses. He stood up to assist Linda in her chair.

"Are you okay?" he studied Linda for a moment.

"I've had better days."

"I'm sorry to hear about your loss," he said genuinely.

Linda dropped her gaze a moment. She twisted the paper napkin in her hand before looking up at him again. "You said you had something that you wanted to tell me?"

"Yes," he straightened in his chair.

"The police were contacted to investigate the death of Steve Mitchell."

"Why?" her eyes widened.

"The hospital officials have reason to believe that his death was a homicide."

"*What?*" She felt a tight feeling in her throat. "Who would want to kill Steve?"

"I'd planned to schedule a meeting with him that night I had him on the phone. The night of his accident. I wanted to see if he had any known enemies or any business dealings that had gone sour, but I never got the chance."

"Do you think it could be the same person who's stalking me?"

"That would be speculation. I—"

"I don't think you'll consider it speculation when I tell you what she said to me on the phone. I remembered. That's why I called you in the first place," she interrupted.

"What did she say?" he questioned.

"She said, 'You're next.' She must have been the one who killed Steve. Otherwise why would she say that to me?"

Detective Andre pondered over the information Linda had just revealed to him. "Doesn't necessarily mean that she's responsible for his death, but I'll take note of it."

Linda took a sip of tea through the lid on her cup. She flipped the lid off the paper cup to stir in some honey. The spearmint scent steaming from the cup was calming, and the light minty flavor was soothing on her dry throat. She had begun to feel stronger. She was determined to cloak herself with strength and courage. She was no longer going to give in to weakness. She needed to find out what had happened to Steve and why. Maybe if she learned the answers to those questions, it would lead to her stalker. She strongly felt that there had to be a connection between Steve's death and her stalker.

"Detective. You said that the hospital has reason to believe that Steve was killed. What was it that made them come to that conclusion?"

"Is this difficult for you to talk about?" He eyed her with concern.

"I'm not going to lie. It's extremely difficult to talk about, but it's necessary. I want to help in any way that I can. I want to solve this case."

"Let's not get ahead of ourselves here. It's my job to solve the case," he chuckled. "You're starting to remind me of someone."

She crooked her eyebrow. "Oh, really? And who might that be?"

"My fiancée, Nicole. She's an investigative reporter. We've worked together here and there on a few cases."

"Hmmm ... interesting. Well, I'm sure she played an important role in cracking the cases."

"I'm going to leave that one alone. I can see where this is going." He laughed quietly.

"To answer your question, the hospital believed that his death was caused by asphyxia." His voice had regained a serious tone.

"Huh? Can you please tell me in English what that means?"

"It means he died by suffocation."

"So how did the hospital determine that it was due to the actions of someone else? Weren't they monitoring him? That's exactly why I went up to that hospital every day, making sure that he was being—"

"Linda, no. The documentation indicated that the staff was doing their job within the guidelines of the hospital."

"Then I don't understand." She placed the lid back on her cup, pressing around it to seal it on.

"One of the staff nurses found a pillow laying very close to his head. It concerned her because when she had checked on him earlier, the pillow was underneath his head and not next to it."

Her thoughts became fuzzy. She couldn't breathe.

"The imprint of the pillow was pressed into his face. The killer must have had to rush out of his room to avoid being seen, and that didn't allow enough time to put the pillow back."

"Oh my God." She thought about how helpless Steve had been as he laid there unconscious while someone smothered him to death.

She caught Detective Moore staring at her with intensity. His expression had become even more serious, and she became uncomfortable under his gaze. Feeling awkward, she looked away.

"There's one more thing that I need to tell you. And I don't know how to tell you this . . . I—"

"What is it?"

"During the investigation into Mr. Mitchell's death, it was confirmed that he was married."

Unable to speak at first, Linda coughed, almost choking on the tea she had just swallowed. Words got caught in her throat. "No way. Uh-uh. I don't believe you." Her heart had been ripped right out of her chest. "Detective, why would you say something like that that's not true? I'm not suffering enough for you? Why would you sit here and tell me this lie? Don't you think that I'd have known if Steve was married?"

He reached across the table and placed his hand

on top of hers, patting it lightly. "Linda? Look at me. I wouldn't make any of this up, and I'm certainly not trying to hurt you. It's unfortunate that sometimes during investigations there is unpleasant information that surfaces."

"Was his wife the family member who claimed his body?"

"I don't know. I suppose so. It would make sense."

She pushed her chair from the table and stood. "Detective, if you don't mind, I don't want to talk about Steve or his wife anymore. If you have no more information about my case, I have to go." Without waiting for him to respond, she grabbed her purse and hurried out of the coffee shop.

28

"I knew it," Carmen sputtered, slamming her hand down on the kitchen counter. "I've always said there was something about that bastard that I didn't like. And God forgive me for calling a dead man a name," she sighed, removing a pot from the drawer and filling it with water.

"You knew he was married?"

"No, but I knew he was hiding something." She glanced over her shoulder at Linda then set the pot on the lit burner. "It just didn't seem right that you had been with him for as long as you have, and he was always so vague with you about his life. You always made excuses for his behavior."

"How could I have known he was married?"

Linda moved to the refrigerator and pulled out a bag of lettuce and a couple of tomatoes. "I've been to his apartment, to his job. There was no indication that he was married. No pictures. Nothing."

"Girl, he was a big, rich executive. He probably has a house in the Hamptons or somewhere upstate and just keeps that apartment in the city for when he wants to fool around."

Linda paused a moment and turned to face Carmen. "I just don't know what to feel—or how to feel," she said. "Now I don't even know what was real and what wasn't real in our relationship."

"Linda, you didn't deserve any of this." Carmen pointed her finger at Linda. "I tell you what. If I were you, I would be mad as hell. I would want to dig his ass up and kill him all over again."

"Carmen."

"I'm sorry, but that's how I feel." She twisted her lips. "How could he get involved with you, knowing that he's married? I bet he has kids, too."

The thought of kids hadn't occurred to Linda. *Oh well, it doesn't matter now. None of it does.* "You and Marc both tried to warn me, but I wouldn't listen to either of you," she replied absently, her mind still holding the thought of Steve possibly

213

having children. "Two years. How could I not know he was married?"

"Because he didn't want you to know. The rich ones are crafty. They have money to play their games."

"But we spent holidays together. How is it possible that he didn't have to be with his wife on Christmas?" Linda replayed those memories in her mind.

Carmen shook her head. "I don't know. "Did Detective Moore say where this wife is?"

"I don't recall. There were so much coming at me at one time. Steve's death is now considered a homicide. He has a wife that I had no knowledge of. I was . . . I just had to get out of there. I didn't want to hear any more about it, so I left."

"Wait a minute. Back up." Carmen's eyes were the size of saucers. "What do you mean Steve's death was a homicide? Somebody killed him?"

"Yes. The hospital is having his death investigated because they think he may have been smothered to death with a pillow."

Carmen held her hand over her mouth in disbelief. "You're kidding me, right?"

"No, I'm not kidding. Why would I kid about

that?" Linda snapped and then shook her head. "I'm sorry, girl. This whole thing has gotten crazy."

"I've said that I want to kill him, out of anger, but you know that I don't really mean anything like that, right?"

"I don't think that you went into his hospital room and killed him."

"The fact that someone would go into a hospital, where there are people working around the clock, to kill someone in their hospital bed seems implausible," Carmen said.

"I know. I'm still trying to wrap my head around it." Linda reclaimed her seat.

"I know this can't be easy on you. First, losing him from what you thought was the result of the car accident. Then finding out that he was married while he was with you. And now finding out he was actually murdered. *Lo siento.* I'm sorry, chica." She patted Linda on the shoulder.

"I just feel so empty and dead inside. There's such a big hole in my heart. A part of me is mourning his loss, and another part of me is so damn angry with him. I'm trying to hate him for lying to me all this time, but—" Her words trailed into a sob.

"Honey, you've been hit with so much. No

wonder your feelings are all tangled. You really should talk to someone about it. Someone who can help you come to terms with all that you're feeling right now."

"I'm not ready to sit down and talk with a stranger about how I'm feeling. Right now, I just want to concentrate on helping the police catch my stalker." She patted her eyes dry with a napkin she lifted from the countertop.

"Hmmm . . . something just occurred to me." Carmen tapped her finger against her lips. "What?" Linda waited for a reply.

"Could the woman who's stalking you be Steve's wife?"

29

Sipping on a white chocolate latte while gazing down at the newspaper, she felt someone standing over her. She looked up to find Detective *fine ass* Sean Gregory smiling his signature smile. He nodded and winked at her. Her eyes rolled up his body and settled on his eyes. He could have easily doubled for Morris Chestnut. His beautiful chocolate skin glistened in the rays of sunlight shining through the coffee shop window.

As he came closer, that woodsy cologne he wore reached her nostrils. Must be that new Calvin Klein cologne. She loved a good smelling man.

He sat across from her, placing his cup of coffee in front of him. His eyes wandered over her tight-fitting blouse. "I'm glad we bumped into each other because it saves me a phone call." His facial expression turned serious.

"What were you going to call me about?" She folded the newspaper and removed it from the table, placing it on her lap.

"I wanted to call you to see how you were doing. I heard what happened with everything surrounding your boyfriend." He shifted in his chair.

"It's sweet of you to be concerned." She cocked her head and smiled, pushing some of her hair out of her face. "I'm doing a whole lot better."

There were a few moments of awkward silence. Once in a while, they would catch one another's gaze and then quickly look away. They both began speaking simultaneously and laughed.

"You go first," they said simultaneously, followed by another round of laughs.

As their laughter abated, she met Sean's gaze. There was something different in the way he looked at her now. The backdrop of voices in the coffee shop seemed to disappear as she focused on his eyes, allowing them to pull her into a trance. He reached over and pushed some tresses away from her eyes, carefully tucking them behind her ear.

His hand still touching her face, he brushed his thumb lightly across her lips, all the while looking into her eyes. Her heart felt like it was going to jump out of her chest. He leaned in closer and lowered his mouth onto hers, and she didn't resist. He deepened the kiss gently, pulling her closer by the nape of her neck.

Confused by what she felt, she broke the kiss. Her belly knotted. She let out a heavy sigh. It scared her that she was drawn to another man so soon after Steve's death. "This is wrong." She stared down at her hands, folded in her lap.

"I'm sorry," Sean apologized, licking his lips as if savoring the taste of her lips. "I shouldn't have."

"It's okay. I'm just as much at fault. I should've resisted." She glanced away a brief moment.

"On second thought, I'm not sorry," he said, sensing her guilt.

"Why would you say that you're—?"

"I'm not sorry because I have feelings for you, Linda." He swallowed.

"But how can you have feelings for me when you don't even really know me? That kiss was wrong. I've just lost my boyfriend. I should be mourning his death, not sitting here kissing someone I hardly know." But she had to admit to herself that she had enjoyed that kiss. Warmth still radiated through her body, stirring up something inside her that she hadn't felt in a very long time.

"I don't want to upset you any more than what you already are, but the man you call your boyfriend was married to someone else. He didn't have the decency to tell you that himself. I won't apologize for the way that I feel about you. I can't explain it, but I've been attracted to you since the first day I saw you."

"What he didn't tell me doesn't discount how I felt about him. I can't just turn my feelings off like a water faucet. I loved him." She stared back at him with an intensity to rival his. It's true that she still felt something for Steve even though he had betrayed her. But she wasn't really sure what it was. Some days it was love, and some days it was hate. She needed to resolve these feelings—feelings for a dead man that she indisputably wasn't going to get any closure from.

"Okay then, tell me you felt nothing at all when we kissed and I'll leave you alone." He rubbed the stubble on his chin, waiting for her to answer.

"I have to go." She had just picked her phone up from the table to stuff in her purse when it rang.

Detective Moore. *Impeccable timing.*

"Hello, detective," she answered, settling back into her chair.

Sean remained seated across from her, watching in anticipation as she conversed on the phone. After a few minutes, she ended the call.

"So what did Andre say?" Sean queried.

"He says there was a break in the case and he has more information to share with me. He's on his way here now." She hung her purse back over the chair.

"Would you mind if I waited here with you?"

"If I said no, I have a hunch that you wouldn't leave anyway," she replied, half-teasingly.

"Your hunch would be correct," he said with crinkled eyes.

They sat and chatted for a while, biding time until Detective Andre Moore showed up. Sean told her about his life and his childhood growing up in Brooklyn and how he became a police officer. She told him about her sheltered childhood and her passion for photography. She had misjudged him from the beginning. He was much different than the egotistic, obnoxious cop she'd thought he was. He seemed to be a warm, kind, and loving person. She had started to feel comfortable being around him. He made her laugh. And that was something she hadn't done in a while.

Detective Moore strolled into the coffee shop and made his way over to their table. He was caught off guard when he saw Sean sitting there. His eyes shifted back and forth, from Linda to Sean.

"Hey, man. I didn't know you were here." He tapped Sean on the shoulder, giving him a secretive, man-to-man look. He grabbed a chair from a nearby table, pulled it up to the table, and sat down to join them.

"I was here when you called." He glanced over at Linda and grinned from ear to ear.

Watching the men exchanging looks—clearly some sort of unspoken boy code—she decided to break in. "Detective, what is it that you came here to tell me?"

"This time, I have some good news to share with you," he said as he smiled, stretching his arms out on the table, his hands clasped together.

"Really?" she sat alert, bracing herself for what he was about to tell her.

"The person who had been stalking you was arrested today. I waited until she was booked and behind bars before I called you."

"Is that all you have to say?" Linda asked, exasperated. "Who is she, and why was she stalking me?" She had waited too long for her stalker to be caught, and she had no more patience. She needed to know more than simply that the woman had been arrested and was in jail.

"Hold on a minute. Let me finish. I just wanted to let you know right off the bat that there had been an arrest."

Sean and Linda both listened intently, waiting for Andre to go on.

Detective Moore straighten up in his chair and continued, "The woman who was arrested for stalking you was none other than Miriam Mitchell, the wife of Steve Mitchell."

"And here's the killer, no pun intended—there's also evidence that she is the one who killed him."

30

Linda couldn't stop thinking about Miriam Mitchell. Not only had that crazy woman stalked her and blown up her car, but she had actually murdered her own husband. This drama was way too much, the stuff cable television movies were made of. And Steve? Married the entire time they'd been dating? How dare he! If he wasn't already dead, she'd kill him herself.

Linda's focus was definitely not on the meeting in which she sat. One of the designers had pulled together an emergency meeting to discuss some last minute changes he wanted made with his new clothing line. The designs had already been lined up for a photo shoot that was to take place in just two days. She smiled absently at the faces around the table—where her full attention should have been—but in addition to the news about her stalker and Steve's evasion of the truth where his wife was concerned, she couldn't stop thinking about that kiss that she and Sean had shared. She kept hitting the rewind button in her head, replaying it over and over, when she felt a light tap on her outstretched forearm.

Even though she had been somewhat startled by the touch, she masked it with a wide grin.

"So tell us, Linda, what are your thoughts about it?" the designer leaned back in his chair, clasping his hands behind his head with a bit of a smirk on his face.

"I'm sorry? Um, *my* thoughts?" pointing her finger at her own chest as redness flushed her cheeks.

"Yep, what are your thoughts about doing the shoot indoors or outdoors?" he hinted, trying to save her from further embarrassment.

She cleared her throat and tried to get her head back in the room. "I'm going to have to agree with the consensus on this one." She prayed that answer would work.

"Are you sure?" He eyed her suspiciously.

Hell no, she thought, but replied, "Yes, I'm sure."

"Okay, then it's settled. The shoot will take place indoors."

Linda released the breath she'd been holding and smiled at her satisfied client.

She felt her phone vibrate inside her purse but decided to wait to check it until after the meeting. She definitely didn't need any more distractions. She had already looked foolish once.

"I just want to thank everyone for coming on such short notice. Does anyone have any questions about what we discussed?" the designer asked as he pushed away from the table. No questions.

While everyone else stood to leave the room, Linda rooted around in her bag for her phone. She had a text message from Sean.

Sean: *Can't stop thinking about you.*

Her heart slammed in her chest. She hadn't felt this giddy since high school when she had a crush on a kid in her chemistry class. She tried to think of a response to send back to him. She typed *me too,* then quickly deleted it. Too predictable. Besides, I don't want to give away that I was thinking about him, too.

Oh really, she typed and pressed the send button.

Sean: *Yes really. Let's meet for dinner?*

Biting her thumbnail and staring down at the text, she mulled over whether or not she should take him up on his offer. It wasn't as if she had other plans. Dinner was going to be a frozen entrée while sitting on the couch with her feet propped up on an ottoman and watching an on-demand movie on TV.

Sure. She pressed send.

Sean: *Great! I'll text you the details.*

31

Marc

He rang the doorbell and waited for her to answer. He knew he should've called first to make sure she was home. He'd wanted to surprise her and had taken a chance on her being in.

"Hey, stranger," he said as he entered Linda's apartment. He watched her face light up with a bright smile. He leaned in and kissed her forehead. "What up, baby girl?" Then took her by the hand and spun her around, his eyes skirting over her from head to toe. "Wow. What are you all glammed up for?"

"I have a date," she said, still beaming.

Marc swallowing hard. "A date?"

"Yes. A date." She sashayed passed him down the hall, making her way to her bedroom. He followed her and watched as she swung open the door to her closet.

"Wait a minute. Isn't it a bit too soon for you to be dating when you just recently lost your boyfriend?"

With her back to him, still rummaging through the closet, she asked, "Why are you concerned about that?" She poked her head out of the closet, briefly eyeballing him. "First of all, you didn't even like Steve, and secondly, it turns out that he really wasn't *my* man to claim."

She sat on her bed, slipping one foot and then the other into a pair of black strappy high-heeled sandals she'd settled on. She stood up and walked over to the silver beveled-edge wall mirror, examining herself from head to toe and turning to view herself from behind. She wore a short, royal blue dress, and her hair was swept up to one side, showcasing the shimmering dangly earrings that adorned her ears.

"So how do I look?" She eyed him in the mirror.

She looked gorgeous. "I think you're making a mistake. But of course, you're not going to listen to me." His words were sharp as a knife.

"What is it with you, Marc? Would you rather see me lying around in misery instead of getting on with my life?" She turned to face him. "Do you realize the hell that I've been through these past several months? I was in a relationship with a married man. I had no knowledge of the marriage, and I was being stalked by his crazy ass wife who tried to kill me and ended up killing him. I would think that you'd be happy for me—happy that I'm getting out and moving on."

"I would be happy for you if it wasn't so soon." His jaw was clenched so tight he was barely able to speak. "Who is this guy anyway?"

"His name is Sean."

"Sean. Where have I heard that name before?" he asked, trying to pull the name from his memory bank, but he couldn't place it.

"He's the detective I met when Carmen was hurt in that car explosion," she reminded him.

"Oh, hell no. You can't be serious?" He'd tried to bite back the bitter words but failed.

"Listen, Marc, I don't know what's gotten into you, but you need to get a handle on it. I don't need your permission to go out on a date. I'm a grown-ass woman. I can pick and choose to date whomever I want to. And if you don't like it, that's your problem." She marched past him, the scent of her perfume lingering behind her.

Marc stood still a moment, allowing her perfume to permeate his nostrils. It was his favorite. Thoughts of this new man, Sean, getting close to her left a stabbing pain in his chest. Taking a deep breath and exhaling it to calm himself, he made his way back to the living room where he found Linda sitting on the plush sofa, filing her nails. He sat down on a nearby chair and leaned forward, elbows resting on his knees. "I'm sorry." His eyes searched her face, seeking forgiveness.

She offered a weak smile and continued to file. The doorbell rang. She stood, smoothed her hands over her dress, and walked to the door. Looking back over her shoulder at him, she said, "This'll be Sean. I suggest you get over yourself. Quickly."

Marc could see a glimpse of Sean as he entered the apartment, wearing a pair of dress pants and a trim-fit, short-sleeved shirt. He heard him greet Linda and saw him bend over and kiss her.

"Mmmm—you even smell beautiful," Sean said.

He caught Sean's glance as he peered over Linda's shoulder. Marc stood as Linda led Sean over to him by the hand. "Let me formally introduce you two," she beamed, her eyes shifting from Marc to Sean. The two of them had already exchanged the once-over look. Releasing her hand from Sean's, Linda said, "Sean, this is my very good friend, Marc." She palmed her hand in his direction. "And Marc, this is Sean," she said, leading with her palmed hand towards Sean this time. He ignored Sean's outstretched hand and nodded curtly. He knew it was ill-mannered, but he didn't care. He could see how uncomfortable it made Linda. She cast him a sideways glance. He shrugged, shoving his hands in his pockets.

"I guess we should get going," Linda said, smiling at the detective.

Marc rolled his eyes and quietly left the apartment alongside of them. His hands tightened into fists as he watched them drive off in the detective's car. He knew now what he needed to do.

32

She gazed out of the car window watching, the scenery and cars swoosh by. It was already late spring, and the days had grown longer. Amber light shined through the clouds in the sky as the sun slowly descended below the horizon. The ride to the restaurant was somewhat quiet as they rode in silence except for the music coming through the car's stereo system. It was a relaxing soul-warming ballad from the R&B artist Kem.

She felt different with Sean than she had when she was with Steve. She almost felt guilty for the sense of comfort she got when around him, as if she was right where she belonged. There was something about his spirit she was connecting with. She couldn't put her finger on it. It was as though their spirits had connected before. Almost like déjà vu.

The silence was broken when Sean asked, "So tell me, what are you thinking about?"

That's the problem—she hadn't been thinking. Because if she had been, she'd have let some grass grow under her feet before she contemplated jumping into another relationship while still trying to get closure on another. *Thinking is the operative word. What the hell am I thinking?*

She straightened up from her relaxed position. Hesitating for a moment, she confided, "Honestly, I'm thinking that this might be a mistake." The words spilled from her mouth so fast she couldn't stop them. She gazed at his profile and watched the one corner of that charming smile that had quickly begun to touch her heart fade. There. She let it out. But why did she feel so guilty for saying it? She'd been through a string of failed relationships. She just didn't see how she could go through another one. Or if she should. Maybe Marc had been right. Maybe it was just too soon.

33

Linda was overcome with emotions. Sean felt so right that she'd thought she couldn't possibly be rushing.

She shifted in her seat uncomfortably, her fingers tugging at the hem of her dress. She looked up at him and smiled. She was tempted to ask him if he had heard her in the car, when she said that this was all a mistake. But she was sure that he had. She decided to leave well enough alone and just enjoy the evening. They sat for a few moments in awkward silence except for an occasional word or two. She was grateful for the interruption when the server returned with their meals.

"To respond to the statement that you made in

the car about *this* being a mistake," pointing his finger from her to him. "I beg to differ." He lifted his fork into his mouth and chewed a bite of food.

She regarded him silently for a moment, gazing into his dark brown eyes and watching a smile curve his lips. "I think that it would be. You don't know me very well. I've had too many heartbreaks, and I'm in a vulnerable state right now where I may be incapable of making good choices. I don't ever want to end up where I am right now—in this same place—again. For God's sake, my last boyfriend was married, and I had absolutely no idea. How could I not have known? Other people were able to see the red flags, but I didn't see a thing."

"I hear what you're saying, and I understand, but you can't live the rest of your life that way. You can't shield yourself from getting to know someone and never open yourself up to love again because of your past relationships." He sipped water from the glass in front of him. His eyes were fixed on hers.

He stood and came around to her side of the booth, sat next to her, and reached for her hand, taking it into his and intertwining their fingers. He slowly lifted her hand to his mouth and gently pressed his lips to the back of it. Feeling his warm breath against the skin of her hand made her tremble. "I promise you that if you give me a chance, you won't need to worry about anything. You will see *no* red flags when it comes to me. I have no secrets and no hidden agenda," he said softly, lips brushing against her hand again. He lifted his eyes, looking her straight in the face.

Damn. He's making this difficult. She couldn't think clearly. Her senses had been heightened by his sensual touch, his silky smooth dark skin, and his masculine musk mixed with the spicy cologne he wore. She had to stop herself from being drawn in by this magnetic force that threatened to take her over mentally and physically.

He tipped her head up with his finger and lowered his mouth onto hers, brushing his lips against hers, teasing her, barely touching them at first. Then he whispered against her lips, "Please give me"— soft kiss—"a chance."

Linda had to admit that she wanted Sean. There was something about him that stirred her soul. But was she willing to throw caution to the wind as she had done in the past? When she thought about it, she had always jumped from one relationship to another without giving herself a break in between. Maybe that was the problem. Was she codependent? Did she need to be in a relationship in order to feel whole? She needed some distance from Sean to find out more about who she was and what she wanted for herself in life.

It took every bit of her self-control and willpower to pull away from his kiss. She breathed in deeply. She knew she needed to say what she didn't want to say. She mentally prepared herself to resist what she knew would be another attempt from him to pursue the idea of them being in a relationship. She slid a few inches away from him in an effort to prevent any further temptation, and she watched his shoulders droop.

She took a quick glance at Sean and then lifted her eyes to the ceiling, attempting to quell her tears, then dropped her gaze back to him. "Sean, I appreciate what you're doing here, but I just can't do this. I'm not ready to be in a relationship right now—with you or anybody else."

"But—"

She reached over and gently pressed her finger to his lips, quieting him. "Please, let me finish." When she was certain he would let her finish speaking, she continued, "I won't be any good to you this way. I need to work on me. I need to process all that has happened in the past several months."

With a short but deep exhale, he ran his hand over his face. "Trust me, I do respect your decision, but I just want you to know that I can help you get through this rough time. You don't have to go through this alone."

"But I *do* have to do this alone. You can't do this for me or with me. No one can."

He was silent for a moment. Appearing unsure of his words, he said, "Okay, I won't push you. I will give you the time that you need to work this out, but promise me one thing?" he asked in a thickened voice.

She was afraid of what he might say. A lump formed in her throat, and she swallowed hard. "What's that?"

"Promise me that you'll come back to me once you've had a chance to sort things out?"

"I'm sorry, but I can't do that. I don't want to give you any false hope."

"Linda, I—"

"I think I should go now. I'll call a cab." She stood to leave.

He pulled at her hand. "No, you won't. I'm not going to let you leave in a cab. I'll take you home.

At least let me do that." His disappointment was palpable, and she felt horrible about it. He signaled the server to bring the bill.

34

The day had arrived for Carmen to leave. She was going back to Cuba to spend some time with her family. Linda was going to miss her terribly. Carmen had become more like a sister to her than a roommate or friend. Especially since she had lived a sheltered life growing up as an only child with no other siblings and not too many friends.

Although she wasn't back one hundred percent to what she had been before the car explosion, she had healed remarkably. She was able to ambulate on her own without assistance, but due to her injury, she walked with a faltering step. Her burns had healed and there were minimum visible scars on her limbs. Linda knew she'd always have the ones on her torso, but the scars on her heart, soul, and memory were probably the worst. There was no escaping those.

The cool evening air gently kissed their faces as they rode with the windows rolled down, the air mingling with the scent of the brand new car Steve had given her to replace the one destroyed in the explosion. Steve enjoyed spending lavishly on her no matter how much she protested. Even if she'd refused his offer of the car, he would have done it anyway—the argument was a no win for her. Carmen, absorbed in her thoughts about seeing her family again, seemed distant. Once in a while, Linda would glance over at her to make sure she was okay, and she'd offer a quickly fading smile in return. Linda could tell she was worried about something. Carmen's face was flushed, muscles tightened. She wasn't good at talking about her feelings. She felt that she always had to hold it together and be strong.

"Are you excited about your trip?" Linda took her eyes off the road briefly, glancing at Carmen once again.

"Yes, but this—" she pointed to herself "—is not the way I expected to return to Cuba." She wiped a tear that had formed in the corner of her eye.

Linda didn't know how to respond. These types of conversations made her uncomfortable. What do you say to someone you look to for strength, someone who always seems confident about themselves, in a situation like this? It had been months now since the explosion, but she would always carry guilt in her heart about what happened to Carmen. She reached over and covered Carmen's hand with hers, squeezing it. "It's going to be okay. I promise you. Your family loves you. *All* of you. Stop stressing."

Carmen twisted a strand of her curly black hair around one of her fingers and smiled. She took in a deep breath and shifted the conversation to a different subject. "I saw Detective Sean the other day." Out of her peripheral vision, Linda could see her friend eyeing her. "He asked about you, chica."

Since that evening in the restaurant, all she had thought about was Sean. As much as she tried to erase him out of her mind, she just couldn't. There was something about him that was different from the others. Why was she so afraid to give in to him? He had called her several times after that evening, but she refused to answer any of his calls. She had been tempted on several occasions, after listening to the recordings of his deep husky voice, but dared not do it. She thought that this was best this way, and over time, he would forget about her. She had too much baggage to bring into any relationship.

Her thoughts were interrupted by Carmen snapping her fingers for attention. "Hey, did you hear what I said?"

"I heard you, but I don't think that the timing is right for me to get involved with someone."

"And why not? Why would you deny yourself a wonderful guy like Sean?"

Linda blew out a breath. "Why are you calling him wonderful? You don't even know anything about him."

"I have a sixth sense about these things. I can smell a rat, and I know a pussycat when I meet one, too."

Linda smirked. "Can we please change the subject?"

"I don't think we have anything more interesting to talk about, and I'm incapable of being quiet."

Linda turned to face her friend again and smiled. "This is exactly why I'm going to miss you."

"This is why everyone misses me." Carmen showed off her dimples. "Now, I want you to tell me why you are torturing yourself—and Sean."

"As I've already explained to him, before I can offer anything to anyone else, I need to work on me first."

Carmen's eyes widened as she straightened up in her seat. "So you two talked about getting together? You've been holding out on me?"

"Yes. We talked, and I told him that I need a break from being in a relationship."

"Are you freaking kidding me? Girl, that man is as fine as they come." She chuckled. "Shoot, give him to me if you don't want him."

Linda glanced at her with a crooked eyebrow. "You mean you don't think that he's a cheater—like all men?"

They both laughed for a few moments. Carmen caught her breath. "They usually are, but not this one. He's the real deal."

They arrived at Kennedy Airport in Queens. Linda stopped the car at the curbside and helped Carmen remove her luggage from the trunk. It was a bittersweet moment for them both. Linda wrapped her arms around Carmen tightly. Tears welled up in both their eyes. Linda wiped Carmen's tears using both her thumbs. "I'm going to miss you so much. Call me when you get there so that I know that you landed safely."

Carmen nodded her head. "I will."

She was already missing her dear friend before she'd even left her sight.

On the drive back home, Linda switched on the radio to fill the car with sound. She had an eclectic taste in music. She listened to a country music station, switched to reggae, then settled on an R&B station. She bobbed her head to the music, singing the words to various songs out loud. She had just finished singing a song by Chaka Khan when that song from Kem came on. The one that was playing the evening she was in Sean's car. She stopped for a traffic light. The song still playing, she closed her eyes and tried to remember every detail about him. The way he moved, the sparkle in his eyes, his masculine scent, his sensual touch, and his deep husky voice.

Honk! Honk! She was startled out of her thoughts by the sound of the cars behind her honking. She didn't realize that the traffic light had turned green.

***

When she turned the key and entered her apartment, an eerie feeling came over her, causing every one of her muscles to tense. She sensed that something was terribly wrong, but she ignored the little voice in her head telling her not to go any further. It was probably just the emptiness of Carmen not being there anymore.

She took a few steps further, her heart racing. She couldn't understand where this feeling was coming from. The apartment was dark inside. She had forgotten to leave a light on. She stretched her arm out into the darkness, searching for the light switch on the wall. If only she had kept that keychain flashlight that Marc had given her in her purse instead of throwing it in her dresser drawer. It certainly would have come in handy tonight. Within seconds, before she was able to reach the light switch, she was grabbed. Her mouth was covered to drown out her scream. She tried desperately to escape from the hold when she felt a cloth pressed over her nose which smelled of fumes. She started feeling dizzy. Then suddenly, everything went dark.

35

Her eyes opened. Her head was throbbing with pain. She couldn't see anything. There was something covering her eyes. She attempted to lift her hand to her head and couldn't. She was sitting in a chair, and her arms were tied behind her back. Her feet were tied together. Panic stirred inside of her. She twisted her hands in a futile attempt to untie them. She was cold. The room smelled musty, like a moldy basement or attic. Her head jerked in the direction of the sound of a faint squeak. Then there was a pitter-patter across the floor. Her heart raced a mile a minute. She was deathly afraid of mice. That creepy-crawly sensation slithered beneath her skin. Anxiety filled her. She worried that the mouse would come near her—or worse, jump on her. She started tapping her feet against the hard floor—cement?— hoping it would deter the little critter from coming any closer.

She needed to think of a way to untie her hands so she could escape. She tried twisting her hands again. Nothing.

She stopped struggling when she heard the muffled sound of keys jingling several feet away, which she figured was where the entrance was. After a few seconds, the door creaked open and shut, and then she heard the click of a light switch. Her chest tightened and her heart raced wildly as she listened to the soft-shoed steps moving closer. Her posture became rigid. Her chest rose and fell with rasping breaths. Sweat beaded on her forehead. She trembled when she felt a rough hand grazing the side of her face. Then lips pressed against her forehead. She was paralyzed with fear.

The stranger did not speak a word.

Immobilized by her terror, the only think that she could do was pray. She prayed silently, *God, please help me. I don't want to die like this.*

She had been praying so hard she didn't realize that he had stepped away from her. She heard what sounded like fingers tapping on some sort of keyboard. Then suddenly a machine-like voice said, "I'm going to ungag you. Don't try anything stupid like screaming, or you'll be sorry." Click. It ended.

She didn't know whether or not she was supposed to nod for an answer. She played it safe and nodded her head to indicate she agreed. Her mouth was freed. She licked her dry cracked lips.

"Who are you? Where am I?" she cried.

Silence.

She felt a cold object touch her lips. She turned her head away from it and pressed her lips together tightly, refusing to give it entry to her mouth. Cold liquid dribbled down her chin.

The recorder came on again.

"I brought you water." Click

Why won't he use his own voice? She was very thirsty. Her throat was as dry as dust. She was tempted. *But what if it's a trick, and it's not water, it's poison? Then again, given a choice, poison may be a better way to go rather than being shot or stabbed to death.* When she felt the object touch her mouth again, this time, she cautiously accepted. The liquid entered her mouth, and she could taste that it really was water. He waited for her to swallow in between spoonfuls.

"Why am I here? What do you want from me?" she questioned after her last swallow. "Please, let me go."

She no longer sensed him near her.

Silence.

She could hear the rattling of paper a few feet away. He was close again. He held something to her nose that smelled like a sandwich–turkey, bacon, cheese. He pushed it against her mouth. She took a bite and chewed. *Why was he feeding her and giving her water?* He offered her a couple more bites.

Then she screamed as loud as her voice would carry, "Help me!" Her skin flushed with pain from the sting of his open hand smacking her face. Her eyes watered. He quickly gagged her again.

He untied her hands and pulled them in front of her, quickly tying them together. He pulled her up from the chair and dragged her over to another area of the room. She calculated it to be only a few steps away. He plopped her onto a low bed. She moaned through the mouth tie, pleading with him to let her go. He loosened the ties on her hand again. She broke one hand free and swung blindly. He grabbed it, shoved her down, and held her to the bed while he pulled one arm up and tied it to a metal bar on the headboard. He threw her feet, which remained tied together, onto the bed, and then tied her other arm to the headboard. She could hear him breathing hard.

The light switch clicked. The door cracked open and then shut. The sound of keys jingled in the door lock.

She lay in darkness. A prisoner. Who had kidnapped her? A troubling thought came to her mind. Could it be that Miriam escaped and is the one responsible for her kidnapping? Maybe that's why she wasn't using her voice. She didn't want her to know it was her. But that thought was crossed out as soon as it came because the person who took her clearly had to be a man. He had the strength of a man and the scent of a man. Maybe there just wasn't any connection at all. If Miriam was her stalker and was locked up for killing Steve and stalking her, then who else would want to hurt her?

36

Sunlight peered through the tiny basement window. She squinted her eyes, adjusting to the glare of the sunlight. The constant rubbing of her head against the bed had loosened the blindfold from her eyes, but her mouth was still tied. She made several attempts to use the same technique to loosen her binding again, but it didn't work. She raised her head from the bed to get a clear view of the room. Just as she thought. She was locked in a basement. The walls and floor were concrete. There were some paint cans stored in a corner. An old wooden ladder leaned horizontally against the wall. Boxes were piled in another corner. The chair she had been tied to was in the middle of the room.

There was only one small, dirty window with iron bars attached on the outside. The room was below ground level, and there was only one door that led out of the room.

She had a burning feeling in her chest. Her stomach ached, and she felt nauseous. The room reeked of urine. She was disgusted with herself. Although there was no one there, she felt ashamed of what she had done. A mouse climbed up on the bed and crawled across the bottom edge of the mattress. She squirmed, kicking her tied-up feet in hopes of frightening it away. The mouse jumped off the bed and scurried across the floor. She lay her head back down and closed her eyes, praying that someone would come and rescue her from this nightmare.

She mulled over the actions of the man who had kidnapped her. It was strange how he had never attempted to harm her physically. Was he holding her for ransom? If he was, that was a joke because neither she nor her family was rich. She was still puzzled by his use of a recording device to give her instructions. *Why not use his own voice?*

She heard a noise outside the window. She lifted her head in that direction and saw the silhouette of a child bending to pick something up. She moaned and thrust her body, attempting to make the bed hit against the wall to make noise. The kid ran away from the window.

Someone was at the door. It was probably him again. The key turned in the lock, and the door pushed open. He didn't immediately reveal himself to her, but she could feel his presence. She stared straight ahead until he came within her view. Her heart stopped. His face froze when their eyes made contact.

I can't believe it! He's come to save me. Thank you, God. Smiling with her eyes, she moaned through the tie around her mouth, gesturing for help.

The bed squeaked as he flopped down on it. His eyes were ice cold as was the smile he flashed.

Her eyes blinked rapidly. Confused by the chilliness of his demeanor, her mind raced, searching for answers. The heat in her body rose. She was burning with anger. Her moans were no longer pleading, they became angry commands.

"Now is that how you respond to someone who's brought you food?" he barked as he held up the white paper bag in his hand. "Maybe I ought to take it back and let your ungrateful ass starve."

He stood from the bed. Her eyes followed him as he walked across the room to retrieve the chair she'd been previously tied to. Linda felt her muscles quiver. A teardrop rolled from the corner of her eye and slid down her cheek.

He returned to the bedside and sat in the chair. His gazed traveled her body and came to rest on her urine-stained clothing. He squared his shoulders. His expression went dark and a muscle in his jaw twitched. "I hate to see you this way, but you left me no choice, baby girl." He let out a short, edgy laugh. "I tried so many damn times to make you see that those fools you fell for wasn't right for you. But would you listen? First, that white boy, and then that punk detective.

In her wildest dreams, she wouldn't have imagined that her kidnapper would be her best friend.

"I'm going to untie your mouth so you can eat. Don't try anything or you're gonna have to answer to this." He reached around under his jacket and pulled out a gun. She had wondered why he was wearing a jacket now that the weather had gotten much warmer.

Her eyes widened. Who was this person? It certainly couldn't be her dearly beloved friend, Marc. Not the Marc she had trusted with every detail of her life. She'd cried on his shoulders so many nights.

He held the gun in one hand while he untied her mouth, then he loosened and untied her hands from the bedrails with the other hand.

She rubbed her wrists in an effort to relieve the numbness that she felt in them from being entwined for hours. "Marc, why are you doing this? I don't understand."

He didn't respond.

"Put that gun away, and let's talk about this," she said, trying to reason with him.

His face and his voice were as tight as a taut rubber band. "Baby girl, you need to understand one thing here. *You* don't call the shots. You better take this serious because I'm not playing any games."

"Will you at least explain to me what the hell this is all about?" Why would you kidnap me and hold me hostage in this rat hole?" Her eyes roamed the dingy basement. "I thought we were friends? You're—you were my best friend. I trusted you. I treated you like a brother, and this is how you show your affection? Have you lost your damn mind?"

He paused for a long moment. "You see, that's the problem. I'm not your brother." He threw the bag with food in it on the bed. "Eat." Nostrils flared.

She pushed it away. "I'm not hungry. I just want you to let me go. This doesn't make any sense."

She dragged her feet up closer to her body and bent over to untie them when she heard a click sound.

"Uh-uh." He shook his head from side to side. "I wouldn't do that if I was you."

"You're not going to shoot me. If you wanted me dead, you would've done it already." She paused and turned her statement into a question in an attempt to get him thinking rationally. "Marc, would you actually shoot me?"

"In a New York minute," his voice stated, steady and calm. "I mean, think about it. Your ass is down here, ain't it?"

She swallowed, wishing his delivery hadn't been so frosty. "If you shoot, someone will hear the gunshot and call the police."

"In this neighborhood, they hear gunshots all the time." He laughed arrogantly. "But just in case, I brought this along." He pulled out a device and attached it to the gun. "This here is called a silencer. Nobody will hear a thing."

She could see that he was dead serious.

"Okay, Marc, what is it that you want from me?" She removed her hands from the rope tied around her ankles and slid her feet back down, rubbing her heels against the bare mattress. "You obviously want something or you wouldn't have gone through the trouble of kidnapping me and bringing me here. You know I don't have money, so what is it?" She spoke through gritted teeth. Heat coursed through her body.

His demeanor shifted a little. For a split second, she caught a glimpse of his eyes softening.

"Why couldn't you just love me?" he spoke quietly.

"What are you talking about? I do—did love you. Like I said before, you're like the brother I never had."

His eyes grew darker, his hands shook. "Stop saying that!" he yelled.

Frightened by his outburst, she swallowed hard. Seeing Marc transform into this hateful stranger really made her uncomfortable.

"I tried to show you many times how much I loved you. But noooo . . . I wasn't good enough. First, it was the white boy—who, by the way, played you because he was already married. I tried to tell you that the bastard was no good, but you wouldn't listen to me. Even Carmen tried to let you know that he was bad for you."

He paused and gazed at her, eyes glassy. Shocked to hear him profess his feelings of love for her, she didn't know how to respond. She kept quiet, thinking it was safer that way. No matter what she would have said, it wouldn't have registered. She was obviously dealing with a sick individual.

He continued, "And now you're all hot and bothered by that cop dude. He's going to hurt you, too." He wiped his runny nose with his jacket sleeve. "We could've been good together."

"Listen to me, Marc. You don't want to do this. What will you gain from holding me here? Do you expect that I'm going to suddenly wake up from this bed one morning and feel the same way about you that you feel about me?" she replied with a scathing look.

She gazed into his eyes, trying to find that kindred spirit she once knew.

He turned away and walked towards the window, still toting the loaded gun.

She stared at the door, calculating how fast she'd have to move to get out and yell for help. She knew it was unlocked because he hadn't turned the lock when he came into the room.

He turned on his heel swiftly as if he had read her mind and held the gun out, pointing in her direction. "Don't even think about it, baby girl." He came closer. "You gonna make me do what I got paid to do in the first place. I spared you because I ended up falling for you when I should've killed you."

37

Left bound yet another day, she closed her eyes and repeated the prayer that she had prayed each day she'd been held captive—for God to spare her life by sending someone to free her. It was the only way she was able to keep her sanity in check. Hearing the squeaking of mice and their pitter patting across the floor unnerved her. Her stomach was queasy, and her heart ran a marathon all day and night. Another sleepless night ahead.

Staring up at the worn dropped ceiling, she thought about all that had happened to her in the last several months—and now this. Another life-shattering blow to her heart and mind. All this time, she had been friends with someone who wanted her dead. How was that possible? Marc had seemed so kind and caring. He was always very protective of her. He'd helped her grow her business. But now she fully understood why he had been overly protective when it came to men. It was because he had feelings for her. Just the thought of that craziness he'd admitted to her made her feel nauseous. Not so much because of the person she had thought he was, but because she now knew that he was a sick individual who wanted to kill her. In hindsight, she saw that their friendship had developed much too quickly, and it was mostly due to his manipulation. She was so busy with her job assignments that having a close friend who helped her and anticipated her needs in almost every aspect of her life without being envious of her had been quite comforting. He'd been better than a personal assistant. Most women would agree that male best friends came with a lot less drama than female friends. And growing up, she didn't have much of a social life, so didn't have any idea of the possible motives behind Marc's being such a good friend to her.

If he were going to kill me, then why hasn't he done it already? This means I still have a chance. She dozed off to sleep, strategizing ways to get Marc to trust her so that she could escape.

* * *

Another day had come and gone. No Marc. She was terrified by the thought that he would leave her there to die. She licked her tongue over her dry cracked lips, trying to moisten them. She swallowed several times to soothe her dry, scratchy throat. She was surprised by the loud sound of her empty stomach growling for food. She tried to force herself back to sleep so that she wouldn't think of food or water. Her body was feeling progressively weaker. Numbness had spread through her hands and feet. What if something had happened to Marc? No one knew she was here. She'd starve to death.

* * *

She woke up groggy, unsure if she was actually hearing her name being called. For a minute, she swore it was Sean's voice. She missed him. Since being imprisoned in the basement, she'd had nothing but time on her hands to think, and he was the only thing on her mind aside from figuring out how to escape. She figured if she died thinking about Sean's voice, it would at least be a more pleasant way to go.

She was interrupted by that voice again, "Linda, can you hear me? Wake up."

She blinked her eyes open. Oh God, was she dead, or was it really him?

Her arms and legs had been untied, but she was too weak to lift them.

"Sean?" she said in a low voice. Her throat was so parched she could barely speak. "Is it really you?"

He smiled down at her. "Yes, it's me. You're going to be alright. Andre is here also. He's calling an ambulance to come and take you to the hospital."

"But how—" Her mind was filled with questions. "How did you know I was here?"

"It's a long story. I'll fill you in on the details once we get you to the hospital and have you checked out."

She didn't have the energy to ask any more questions. She was too weak for it. She closed her eyes again and thanked God from the depths of her heart that Sean was here. She wasn't going to die in this rat hole.

38

The last thing that she wanted to do was to lie down on a bed to rest. When Sean brought her home from the hospital, she wanted to sit up on her couch and watch TV. She would've stayed outdoors for a while longer, but she was still feeling a little weak. She had showered and put on a pair of sweat pants and a T-shirt while Sean installed new locks on her apartment door. While in the car, she had tried to get him to tell her the details of how he found her, but he wanted to wait until they were back at her place and settled in so that there would be no distractions.

She came out of the kitchen carrying two glasses of iced lemonade. Sean had finished installing the new locks on the door and was seated on the couch, watching her as she neared him.

Smiling, she offered him one of the glasses. "I hope you like lemonade."

He took the glass from her and smiled back. "Yes, and it couldn't have come at a better time. I'm thirsty!" He took a few sips from the glass before setting it down on the cocktail table in front of them.

She sipped her lemonade and gazed at him a moment. She hadn't noticed his thick lashes before. He slid closer to her and took her hand in his, caressing it softly, absently circling his finger inside her opened palm which sent chills of pleasure through her body. "I don't know what I would've done if I had lost you." His dark brown eyes stared at her so intently that she wondered if he could see right to the depths of her soul.

She lowered her eyes and gently withdrew her hand from his. She didn't know how to respond. She rubbed the back of her neck. It was all that she could think of to do with her hand at the moment. She turned to him, avoiding direct eye contact for fear of falling victim to the desire that was stirring up inside her. "Sean, you said that you were going to tell me how you knew where to find me?"

He leaned back into the soft, cushioned couch, deliberating what to say. "A few days ago, I got a call from Carmen. She said that she had tried to reach you several times and had left a few voice messages. She thought it was very unlike you not to return her calls, especially since you were expecting a call from her the day that she left for Cuba. She also tried calling that guy Marc, who also didn't answer her calls." Linda's body tensed at hearing Marc's name mentioned.

Sean noticed her reaction. "I'm sorry. Are you sure you want me to continue?"

She nodded her head.

"Carmen got worried and called me. I tried contacting you as well, but I thought that you weren't returning my calls because—well—because of our last conversation." He paused briefly. "I remembered that lady Gladys who came up with me to your apartment the day of the car incident, and I asked Carmen to call her to have her go check on you. I would've gone over myself, but I wouldn't have handled the rejection well if you had been there." He watched her for a reaction, but she gave nothing away. "Anyway, Gladys told Carmen that when she was taking her trash to the incinerator, she saw a man that fit

Marc's description going into your apartment. She said that she didn't think anything of it at first, until another neighbor reported to her that she saw that same man carrying you down the stairs. When she asked him why he was carrying you, he mumbled something about you being sick."

Linda interrupted, "How did you or whoever figure it was Marc and not someone else?"

"Carmen remembered that you had given him a key to the apartment to use in case there was some sort of an emergency. When Gladys described the man that she had seen entering the apartment, Carmen immediately thought it was probably Marc. She was disturbed by the idea of him carrying you out. She thought that to be a bit odd. It didn't sit right with her, so for that reason, she asked me to look into it."

Linda shook her head from side to side in disgust at herself for trusting him. Giving Marc that key turned out to be a huge mistake that almost cost her life. Actually, befriending him, period, had been a grave mistake.

"A friend of mine who's a private investigator owed me a favor, and I called it in. He worked on this together with Andre," Sean continued.

"I don't understand. Why didn't someone rescue me sooner?" Her eyebrows met in a frown.

"The private investigator couldn't make an arrest. He's only allowed to make a citizen's arrest—and only in some cases. He didn't want to mess up and scare Marc off, so he waited and brought Andre with him on one of his stakeouts, which was when Marc came out of an abandoned house in Brooklyn, shoving what seemed to be a gun in his waistband. Although Andre desperately wanted to go into the house to take a look around, he couldn't without a search warrant. And it took nearly twenty-four hours to get a damn warrant." He leaned forward. "Once he got the search warrant, that's when we combed the house and found you."

"When Marc didn't come back—not that I wanted him to—I was afraid he had left me there to die."

"No telling what he would've done had he come back. Especially since he had a gun on him. I can't believe that crazy dude's been around you all this time, calling himself a friend of yours. I knew something was up with him that day that I came to pick you up. I couldn't put my finger on it, but something was definitely off about him."

"He said something very peculiar before he left me the last time. It makes the hairs lift on my neck every time I think about it."

"What did he say?" he steeled himself.

"He said he should've done what he was paid to do, and that was to kill me," she murmured.

His phone rang. He detached it from his waist and answered the call. The whole while he was talking into the phone, his eyes were fixed on her. He pressed a button to end the call. "That was Andre. Marc's being arraigned. You don't have to attend if you don't want to. That's your call."

"What happens if I don't go?"

"Whether you go or not, the judge will let him know what he's being charged with and will set bail."

Her eyes widened. "What? You mean he's going to be released to come after me again?"

He pulled her into his arms. "He's not getting out, Linda. Even if he's charged with a lesser crime, I won't let anything happen to you. I just thought you could get some answers. Some closure. You called the man your friend. He had a key to your apartment. You need to see him again and find out why he did the things he did."

Linda swallowed and pulled herself out of his

273

arms. She let out a long sigh. "I guess you're right. I do. I just—" She hesitated and looked away from his eyes. "I didn't think it would be today."

"The arraignment was moved up. I'm sorry for the short notice."

She smiled through twisted lips and nodded. "I guess I should go and get dressed."

Sean dropped his serious expression, and his arresting eyes relaxed her.

39

Linda needed to do something to ease the empty feeling in the pit of her stomach. At his arraignment eight months ago, Marc had been charged and his trial date scheduled. Those months had flown by, it seemed, and now a part of her wanted to back out of attending Marc's trial. Sean thought that it was a good idea for her to be there so that she could bring some closure to what had happened. He'd been her rock since the day he found her locked away in that dingy basement.

She decided to go for a long walk. After donning Capri shorts and a T-shirt, she bent to tie the laces of her sneakers. Then she grabbed her keys and headed out the door.

The sky was filled with an array of clouds. The light waves of wind splashed against her face as she walked briskly along a trail through Central Park. There weren't many people along her trail, but every now and then, she would encounter someone jogging past her. As she made her way back to the front of her apartment building, she saw Sean standing there, anticipating her arrival.

"Hi. What are you doing here?" She felt her cheeks flush.

"Did you think I would let you walk into that courtroom alone?" He grinned as if he could see her sudden embarrassment.

"I guess you kinda caught me off guard. I didn't expect to see you here," she said, recollecting the time first time he had seen her looking like a hot mess when he and Detective Moore had waited for her outside her apartment building.

"Don't worry about it. You look cute. Maybe a bit on the smelly side, though." He pinched his nose. "But nonetheless—"

She playfully punched his arm and giggled. She was actually glad to see him. She wasn't sure how'd she feel facing Marc. She knew it wasn't going to be easy, but she wanted to get it over with. She needed to put it all behind her.

* * *

Linda felt her palms moisten as she sat on the wooden bench next to Sean in the courtroom. When Detective Moore entered the courtroom, Sean turned and gestured for him to come join them. He strolled down the row of benches and positioned himself on the other side of Linda.

"Nervous?" Detective Moore glanced down at her.

"I'm fine," she lied. She was a nervous wreck. This would be the first time that she would be face to face with Marc since he'd held her captive in that basement. She had changed her mind and backed out of going to his arraignment. She could feel her stomach rolling while she waited for the proceedings to take place.

"Don't be anxious. Everything is going to be fine. There's enough evidence to put him behind bars for a very long time." Detective Moore patted her hand.

She bit down on her lips, praying that the detective was right. The thought of Marc being free anytime soon was terrifying. Where could she go? Where could she hide? She was a photographer. Her name was her brand. She was too easy to find. She shook her head and closed her eyes. She hated that she even had to think about such a thing as hiding or running. She hadn't done anything wrong. Steve's lies had brought all this drama to her door and into her life. She wished he was alive, not only because she hated how he'd died, but because she wanted so badly to tell him how she felt about her heartache.

More people had filled the courtroom. Then she saw Marc being escorted into the room by someone she presumed to be his lawyer. She glanced around the courtroom and spotted Gladys sitting a few rows behind them. She wondered why she was there, but then realized that she was the one who had seen Marc enter her apartment. The court must have subpoenaed her to come. She offered her a smile and waved her hand.

Linda's interaction with Gladys was interrupted by the booming voice of the bailiff instructing them to stand for the judge's entrance. The judge was a stocky woman who appeared to be in her late fifties. She entered the courtroom swiftly and claimed her seat. The proceedings began.

Linda was asked to come forth, and she fielded questions from both the prosecuting attorney and Marc's lawyer. She started quivering and felt faint when she had to identify Marc, only making the briefest of eye contact with him.

Gladys was also asked to identify Marc. She didn't seem a bit nervous. She boldly pointed to him and said, "That's the man right there that I saw going into Linda's apartment." Before being escorted from her seat, she continued, "You should be ashamed of yourself."

Sean lifted Linda's hand and rested it on his lap intertwining their fingers while they listened as the case continued.

The prosecutor, a tall, thin, and bald man, strutted up to Marc, who had taken a seat on the stand, and asked with a booming voice, enunciating each word clearly and confidently, "Is it true that you were institutionalized in a mental hospital and were being treated for a psychotic disorder?"

Marc paused before he answered yes.

"Is that where you met Miriam Mitchell and conspired with her to kill her own husband in cold blood?" the prosecutor continued.

Marc didn't speak.

"Answer the question," the prosecutor demanded.

"My client was not responsible for the death of

Steve Mitchell," Marc's lawyer objected to the question. "It's a fact that his wife was the sole perpetrator. She was identified and has been charged with his murder."

"Mr. Wilson, tell us where you met Ms. McNair and what your relationship with her was," the prosecutor stated.

Linda watched Marc closely. He was becoming agitated and angry. He shifted in his seat and tugged at his tie. He was taking a long time to respond. His jaw tightened as he stared down at her. She, in response, tightened her grip on Sean's hand. She couldn't wait for this to be over. She almost wished she hadn't come.

"I loved her," he said through gritted teeth.

"Are you telling me that you and the victim," the prosecutor pointed to her, "had a love affair? I'm confused."

"No. She had less than stellar taste in men. She had an affair with a married white man—and then that two dollar cop—over me."

Linda felt like a sharp knife had just ripped through her heart, hearing Marc speak of her that way.

"Mr. Wilson, please answer the question?"

Marc settled back in the chair, pondering what

he was going to say. Then he broke down and sobbed, "I didn't want to hurt her. She was sweet to me. I wasn't supposed to have fallen for her." He wiped his face with his hands.

"Can you explain to the court what you mean by that?" The prosecutor waved a hand toward the jury.

Marc sniffled, reached into his pocket, and pulled out a handkerchief and blew his nose into it. "When I was about to be discharged from the hospital—"

"This was no ordinary hospital, Mr. Wilson, was it? It was an inpatient mental health institution!" he bellowed.

Marc's attorney stood up. "Objection, your honor. Counsel is badgering my client."

"Your honor, the type of hospital that Mr. Wilson was admitted to is relevant to the case," the prosecutor replied.

"You may answer the question." The judge looked down at Marc.

"Yes. It was a hospital for inpatient mental health. As I was saying, I was being released, and I met this lady who said that her husband was rich, and she wanted to hire me to do a job for her. She had found out somehow that her husband had been cheating on her with another woman while she was in the hospital," he paused. "I didn't believe her at first, but then she showed me proof of who he was. I needed the money because I had lost my job while in the hospital, and I didn't have any money to pay my bills. I was desperate. When I met Linda that night at the gallery, it wasn't by accident."

"This lady you're referring to—what's her name?" the prosecutor probed.

"Miriam Mitchell."

"What kind of job did Ms. Mitchell want you to do? Kill her husband and then Ms. McNair?"

Marc's attorney sprung from her seat. "Objection, your honor. Counsel's leading my client."

"Objection sustained." The judge narrowed his eyes at the prosecutor. "Rephrase your question, counselor."

"Mr. Wilson, can you tell the court what was it that Ms. Mitchell paid you to do?" He walked away from Marc to face the jurors.

Marc put his head down a moment then lifted it again. "She paid me to stalk Linda and to use whatever means necessary to stop her from seeing her husband."

Linda felt sick. She looked from Sean to Detective Moore, both of whom seemed less than stunned by Marc's admission. She surmised they—especially Detective Moore—dealt with lawbreakers and nuts like Marc every day. Miriam hadn't been her stalker. All this time, her stalker had been right up under her nose. She wiped the perspiration from her forehead. The nausea in the pit of her belly was increasing.

"Even if stopping her meant to kill her?" The prosecutor turned back to face Marc.

"Objection," Marc's attorney called out.

"Overruled," the judge responded.

"No more questions, your honor."

40

With each click of her heel on the glossy, waxed floor, her heart pounded. She had to do it. She had to see him one last time. She needed more answers. When the correction officer opened the door to the room, she began to tremble. There was Marc, sitting behind a glass partition. This time in his orange jail jumpsuit. His eyes rolled over her as she came closer. Linda released her held breath slowly and sat down facing him. His eyes remained fixed on her.

Her hands shook as she lifted the phone receiver attached to the wall. She waited until he had done the same before she began to speak.

Clearing her throat, she said, "I—I need to know why."

He lowered his eyes and then lifted them back to hers. "I'm sorry."

"I didn't come here for your apologies, Marc. I came to get closure." She blinked back tears. "Did you know about the bomb?"

"Honestly, I didn't." His chest rose and fell as he inhaled and then exhaled a deep breath. "Not at first anyway."

"What do you mean, not at first?" She leaned in closer, pressing the phone tighter against her ear so as not to miss a word.

"I didn't know until after it happened. She—Miriam—claimed to have seen Steve at some jewelry store. She believed he was buying a gift for you. She also knew about the car that he'd bought you." He shifted in his seat.

"How did she know about that?"

He waited a beat. "Because I told her." His head was down, but his eyes looked up at her. "I didn't know that crazy bitch was going to blow it up. She was some kind of engineer before she went into the hospital. I guess that's how she knew how to make one."

Linda dismissed it. She didn't care about

Miriam—she wanted to know about Marc. "You—you pretended to be my friend. I . . ." the words trailed off as she ran her hand down her face.

"Linda, I was— I got mad at you . . . and . . . you see, I wasn't well. Remember that time I called you and said I had to leave town for a few days?"

She frowned as she waited for him to continue.

"I didn't leave to visit relatives. I checked myself back into the hospital. I couldn't handle my feelings for you. You just reminded me so much of her."

"What the hell are you talking about?" She stared at him incredulously.

"My ex-girlfriend. You're the spitting image of her," he continued. "The reason why I was hospitalized in the first place is because she and I had an argument. She was backing away from me, and she fell down a flight of stairs."

"What?" Linda couldn't believe what she was hearing. "Where is she now?"

"She's dead." A teardrop slid down his cheek. "They arrested me because they thought I'd killed her. But I didn't do it. It was an accident." He shook his head. "I never would have hurt her."

Linda stared at him blankly, not knowing whether or not to believe him.

"Her death sent me over the edge." He sniffled. "My lawyer arranged for me to be institutionalized so I could get help rather than be sent to prison for a crime I didn't commit."

She willed herself not to feel sorry for him. There was still more she needed to know.

"You said that our meeting wasn't by chance? Explain," she interjected.

He straightened up in his chair and appeared to be gathering his thoughts. "To add to what I already said in the courtroom, Miriam somehow knew that you'd be there. She gave me a picture of you. When I saw your picture, I just couldn't believe how much you looked like—"

"One more question. Were you planning to kill me if the cops hadn't got to you first?"

Another tear rolled down his cheek. "I—I—" He placed the phone back on its cradle and pushed away from the table.

Linda watched as he left the room. She sat quietly for a few moments before she stood up to leave. He had really been going to kill her.

41

The last box was loaded onto the moving truck. After she'd watched the truck drive away, Linda went back up to her apartment to take one last look around. The place held so many memories for her—good ones and, more recently, very bad ones. She needed a fresh start. There were too many reminders here of the times she had shared with Marc. Times when he'd comforted her, times when they'd celebrated, and the time when he'd kidnapped her. Even though Marc was in jail, she no longer felt completely safe there. She missed Carmen. Her lips curled into a smile as she passed what used to be her friend's bedroom. Carmen had decided to extend her stay in Cuba, and she didn't know when she might be returning to the States again. She planned to send for the rest of her things at a later date.

The heels of her shoes echoed in the empty apartment as she ventured from room to room, pausing at the flashes of each memory. Her cell phone chimed, and she could feel it vibrating in the purse slung over her shoulder. She took it out but didn't recognize the incoming number.

"Hello."

"Ms. McNair, My name is Chris Powell. You don't know me. I'm a friend—I mean, Steve was a friend of mine, and I was also his attorney."

Surprise resonated in her tone. "Um, how can I help you?" Needing some additional support, she leaned against the kitchen island and waited for what was coming next.

"I'm sorry it took so long to get in touch with you. I'd been meaning to call, but it kept slipping my mind until I read about your case recently in the newspaper."

"Go on." She shrugged her shoulders even though he was unable to see.

"Would it be possible for you to meet me in my office today? There's something I think you should know."

Linda hesitated. "Couldn't you just tell me over the phone?" She had no idea what he could possibly have to say to her, and she didn't want to wait to hear it.

"It's complicated, and I really don't feel comfortable discussing it over the phone. I'd prefer to tell you in person," he stated. "It won't take much of your time."

"I don't mean to offend you, but if you read about my case in the newspaper, then I think that you should understand that my trust level is at an all-time low."

"Quite understandable. How about you bring someone with you? You don't have to come alone."

She pondered this. She *was* curious to know what it was that he felt was so important for her to know. "Let me think about it and get back to you."

He gave her his office address, a number where he could be reached, and ended the call.

"Hmmm . . ." She tapped her finger against her chin while still holding the phone in her hand. "What was that all about?"

She strolled through the numbers in her phone until she reached Sean's number and tapped the screen. Her nerves were in a flurry, and she began twisting her hair around her finger while she waited for him to answer, anticipating the sound of his deep, husky voice. He had the kind of voice that would make a girl drop her— Her thoughts were interrupted when he answered the phone.

"Hello, Sean. I just received an interesting call."

"Don't tell me that that fool is calling you from jail?" he groaned.

"Oh no. Nothing like that. Steve's attorney friend called and said that he wanted to talk to me."

"About what?" His voice sounded skeptical.

"I don't know. I assume it's something about Steve. He requested a meeting at his office."

"I don't like the sound of that. Why can't he tell you over the phone?"

"I've already had that discussion with him, and he's not budging. Listen, I called you to ask if you could come with me or meet me at his office."

* * *

Sean was already waiting in the lobby of the building when she arrived. They took the elevator up to the tenth floor. Before they walked through the door of the office suite, Sean grabbed her hand and asked, "Are you sure you want to do this?"

She took in a deep breath. "Yes. Whatever it is, maybe it will bring some closure."

They were greeted by a cheerful, blond-haired woman upon entering the reception area of the upscale office.

They sat side by side on the soft brown leather sofa, waiting for Steve's lawyer. Linda wrung her hands and tapped her foot, her nerves getting the best of her. Sean placed a hand on top of hers and smiled warmly at her. She immediately felt calmness take over. She was just beginning to relax when a handsome man who appeared to be in his early thirties approached them, smiling brightly. They both stood. The man extended his hand to her. "I'm Chris. You must be Linda?"

She nodded and pointed to Sean. "This is Sean. You said it was okay to bring someone with me."

He shook Sean's hand and greeted him as well.

Sean turned to her. "I'm going to wait right here for you."

"Don't you want to come in with me?" she questioned.

"I think this is something you need to do on your own."

She followed Chris down the corridor into his office. It elaborately and tastefully decorated, definitely an indication of his success. He motioned for her to sit down in the leather chair in front of his desk.

"Can I get you anything?" he asked.

"No, I'm fine" she said, leaning forward in the chair, quirking an eyebrow, and smiling. "If you don't mind, I would just like to get to the point of why I'm here."

"I've kept you waiting long enough, haven't I?" He laughed softly. He moved to the chair behind his desk and sat down, leaning forward to rest his forearms on the desktop. "Again, I apologize for not getting in touch with you sooner. I'm sorry that I didn't get the chance to meet you when Steve—" he dropped his eyes and then lifted them again "—when he was alive. Anyway, the newspapers made him out to be some sort of husband out gallivanting and cheating on his wife while she was locked away in a mental institution. But that wasn't how he was at all."

"Really? How do you explain it?" She bit the inside of her lips, narrowing her eyes at him.

"Miriam was getting better—or so we thought. I had drawn up the divorce papers and had them served to her. Steve was determined to take his relationship with you to the next level." He pulled out a small blue velvet box wrapped in a white ribbon bow from his desk drawer and handed it to her. "He'd bought this for you. You were all he talked about, Linda. I want you to know that because *he* would have wanted you to know that, and he would have wanted you to have this."

She carefully untied the ribbon and opened the box. Inside was a sparkling princess cut diamond engagement ring. She closed the box and wiped away the tears that had just filled her eyes. Her mind swirled dizzily, and her heart wasn't faring any better. The ring was beautiful, but it couldn't replace the pain of betrayal. She tried to repress the images of Steve and Miriam, but she couldn't. "This doesn't excuse the fact that he didn't share the fact of his marriage with me. He took away my choice. He didn't let me decide whether or not I wanted to get involved with a married man. Which, by the way, I wouldn't have done if I had known."

"I understand your disappointment. He went through a very tough time with Miriam when their daughter died. She accused him of killing their daughter."

For a split second her breathing stopped. She gripped the arms of the chair she was sitting in. "Steve has—had—a child? He killed her?"

"He had a child, and no, he didn't kill her."

"Then what happened to her?"

He cleared his throat. "She died from a childhood disease. Measles, I believe it was."

"But they have vaccines for that. I didn't even know kids still got measles in this country."

"Steve was against having her vaccinated. He believed it caused autism. His sibling became autistic after having it, and his parents blamed it on the vaccination. Miriam went along with his decision to not vaccinate their daughter, but then she became ill with the disease and had no protection against it. Miriam couldn't handle the loss of her child. She blamed Steve and had a mental breakdown."

Her thoughts turned to Steve. Her feelings were still ambivalent, but it must have been tough on him to lose his daughter and watch his wife deteriorate right before his eyes.

Chris continued, "I just wanted you to know the whole story. I didn't think it would be an appropriate conversation to have over the phone, so I'm glad you took time to come."

"I appreciate you reaching out to me."

"He was a stand-up guy. He was my friend, and I wanted you to know that you meant something in his life. I didn't want you to feel like he was that stereotypical guy who cheated on his wife. His marriage ended long before he met you. His situation was complicated, and he tried to make the right decisions. Unfortunately, he fell short of being honest with you about it."

She had to admit to herself that the meeting with Chris had finally brought closure to some unresolved questions she had about Steve.

* * *

When they reached the lobby of the building, Sean wrapped his arm around her waist, pulling her closer to him. "Come home with me," he spoke softly into her ear in that sexy, husky voice.

Her breath caught. Her knees weakened. There was a serious battle going on between her heart and her brain. "I really should get to my new place and do some unpacking." She glanced up at him and smiled.

"How about if I come over later and help you?" He rested his hand on the small of her back, leaned in, and brushed his lips against hers.

She licked her lips, tasting the sweetness he'd left behind.

* * *

This was the first time she'd been in Sean's

apartment. She glanced around, admiring the colorful artwork and the various sculptures. "I had no idea that you had an eye for art," she said as she watched him pop open a bottle of wine.

He looked up at her with his signature crooked grin. "I've been known to collect a few pieces here and there." He handed her a glass of wine.

They lifted their glasses simultaneously to their lips, each taking a sip. He set his glass down. His gaze hovered on her lips. His finger lightly traced the trembling line of her lower lip. He treated her neck to a flurry of soft, featherlike kisses, then returned to her earlobe and nibbled it gently. He opened his mouth, gently breathing warm air into her ear. A low moan escaped her when he pulled her closer to him and pressed his hardness against her. He brushed his lips against hers then parted them with his tongue and deepened their kiss. His hand slid under her skirt, following the path up her thighs till it rested between her legs and his finger slipped inside her silk panties to explore her love cave. She panted. She could hardly contain her excitement from his touch. She wanted him. He released her long enough to do something that she initially found peculiar. He grabbed a glass and filled it with ice cubes, then took her by the hand

and led her into his bedroom. He kissed her long and passionately before he eased her down on the bed. He undressed her, sliding her skirt and panties down, then pulling her blouse over her head and slowly unfastening her bra. She could see his manhood growing as his eyes roamed over her naked body. He reached for the glass of ice, took a cube out and placed it in his mouth then lowered his mouth onto hers. He prompted her to take the ice cube into her mouth, and they passed it back and forth a couple of times until he ended up with it in his mouth. He moved slowly down, planting alternately cool and warm soft kisses along the length of her body, the ice cube in his mouth. His lips closed around her nipple, teasing with his tongue, sucking and making quick nips, occasionally letting the ice touch it and sending her into a frenzy of arousal. She writhed under his mouth. She eagerly parted her legs, and he dipped his head, alternating between lightly touching her clit with the ice and using his mouth and tongue. Waves of pleasure sent her body into spasms. Her legs trembled, and her breathing became unmanageable. Cries of inexplicable joy escaped her lips. She heard herself speaking words she couldn't even understand. He continued to lightly touch her with the ice, licking and sucking, sending her over the edge. She was moaning and screaming, calling out his name. He withdrew his tongue, moved upward, and swiftly tore open a condom package with his teeth. He rolled the condom over his erection. They held each other's eyes as he lowered his body onto hers, entering her slowly, inch by inch. She raised her hips, matching his rhythm, undulating until they reached the peak of ecstasy. He muffled her cries with deep kisses. They had become one.

Exhausted from several rounds of lovemaking, they lay in bed, her head resting against his chest and her leg thrown over one of his. He lifted her chin with his finger and gazed into her eyes. "I love you, and I want you to be a part of my life for the rest of my life."

A teardrop fell from her eye. No other man had ever made her feel the way Sean had. She didn't want to have feelings for this man so soon, but the truth was that she did.

"Is that a teardrop I see?"

Teardrops know my name, she thought. As she snuggled in his embrace, she knew deep down that she belonged with him, and he would be hers forever.

The End

Thank you for reading!

Author's Note

Dear Reader,

I hope you enjoyed Teardrops Know My Name. As an author, I love feedback. So tell me what you liked, what you loved, even what you hated. I'd love to hear from you. You can write me at daliafloreabooks@gmail.com and visit me on the web at daliafloreabooks.com.

I need to ask a favor. If you're so inclined, I'd love a review of Teardrops Know My Name. Loved it, hated it. I'd just enjoy your feedback.

Reviews can be tough to come by these days. You, the reader, have the power now to make or break a book.

Thank you so much for reading Teardrops Know My Name and for spending time with me.

In Gratitude,
Dalia Florea

Author's Note

About the Author

Dalia grew up in Queens, New York and now makes her home in Northern Virginia outside of Washington, D.C. Her debut *Mirrored* reached the Top 100 Bestseller's list in Women's Detective Fiction. She is a voracious reader who enjoys writing fiction stories with a mixture of mystery, suspense, and romance. When she isn't crafting suspense romance, she enjoys reading, attending live music concerts, and visiting wineries. Visit her at www.daliafloreabooks.com